Am I a Monster?

J. Boote

Copyright © 2023 by J. Boote
All rights reserved.

No part of this book may be reproduced in any form or by any electronic or mechanical means, including information storage and retrieval systems, without written permission from the author, except for the use of brief quotations in a book review.

This is a work of fiction. Names, characters, places, and incidents either are the product of the author's imagination or are used fictitiously. Any resemblance to actual persons, living or dead, events, or locales is entirely coincidental.

Formatting by Red Cape Publishing.

Cover art by Maisie Stokely.

Contents

Author's Note	4
Chapter 1	5
Chapter 2	10
Chapter 3	15
Chapter 4	20
Chapter 5	24
Chapter 6	35
Chapter 7	39
Chapter 8	52
Chapter 9	59
Chapter 10	65
Chapter 11	75
Chapter 12	85
Chapter 13	92
Chapter 14	103
Chapter 15	115
Chapter 16	120
Chapter 17	130
Chapter 18	137
Chapter 19	148
Chapter 20	154
Chapter 21	159
Chapter 22	163
Chapter 23	169
Chapter 24	176
Chapter 25	182
Chapter 26	187
Chapter 27	191
Chapter 28	194
Chapter 29	202
Author's Notes	207
Also Available	211

Author's Note

The book you are about to read is extreme horror. This means there are some graphic scenes of SA and torture involved. If animal abuse is a problem, you're fine! None of that happens here. If this is not your thing, close this book right now and walk away. I don't want to see you complaining about being offended or shocked on social media or logging complaints on Amazon. You have been fairly warned.

Chapter 1

Sarah's body was broken, quite literally. She wasn't sure if there was a single bone left in her that wasn't snapped, cracked, or chipped in some way. Not even the toes on her feet. She had to drag herself across the room and even her elbows howled in agony. She guessed they were both chipped from repeated abuse. Sarah wasn't sure if it was more painful to shuffle on broken feet and risk collapsing or just grit what remained of her teeth and pull herself along. If pain could be measured in some way scientists would have to find yet another method of measuring hers—it would go far and beyond any scale currently available. She figured she should be dead already by now and countless times had begged for such an eventuality, but that would have been too easy. God wouldn't allow such an occurrence yet.

As she pulled herself across the carpet, she could feel layers of skin peeling off, left behind, as though shedding a skin. And in a way she was—the trouble was that in her condition there was very little likelihood of another replacing it. Red, raw flesh remained instead, infected in many places that gnawed and bit at her nerve endings, down to the bone even. It was as if the carpet was made not from soft fibres, but needles, each one prodding at her malnourished, dying body. But she refused to give up, not after all she had endured. Not when escape was finally possible, within the grasp of broken fingers, after so long. That was a greater torture than anything she had been subjected to so far, which was a lot; the chance of freedom so terribly close she could taste it almost. At least she would if her tongue retained any taste buds, which was questionable.

Am I a Monster?

The person across the room from her was also in considerable pain. Not as much as she was, she didn't think, but the groaning coming from him suggested it wasn't a great deal less. Not yet anyway, but she was going to fix that, if it was the last thing she ever did. She refused to die until she heard him scream and howl with everything he had. He was going to shit himself just as she had on so many occasions. Maybe she'd force feed him it too, so he knew what it was like.

On the table beside his writhing body was a vase, full of pretty red roses. A gift to the guy's girlfriend, she thought. Grimacing, sweating, she managed to pull herself onto one elbow, that was surely about to snap in half at any second and took one flower from the vase. One was more than enough for what she had in mind. This present was going to backfire on him in ways he could never imagine.

Gritting her teeth, she pulled herself closer to him, every movement sending shockwaves down her body, bolts of lightning that rattled her broken bones. She was pretty sure she was losing blood somewhere too, perhaps her vagina which wouldn't be surprising, so if she was to make her way out of this alive, somehow, she had to hurry.

The naked boy saw her coming and tried to sit up, but he was in too much pain to make any kind of progress escaping her—severe concussion must surely be causing intense dizziness. Seeing the fear and hatred in his eyes spurned her on, a drug she was inhaling, airborne. Sarah reached him and tried to climb up his legs so she could use her bodyweight to pin him to the floor. He lashed out but his efforts were weak. His kneecaps collided with her ribs, and she hissed, too tired to scream which is what had been her intention. She had an idea all her ribs were broken by now, not just the odd one here and there. His left kneecap rubbed against her torn vagina, and she gasped for air, all of it taken from her lungs. It felt like she'd just been kicked there. Again. But finally, she made it.

"I hope it hurts," she managed, blood dripping from what remained of her lips. "It's nothing compared to what I have in mind, though."

"Fuck you, bitch," he spat. "He'll be back any second and you'll be begging for him to kill you again. Just like before. But it's not gonna happen. I'll personally slice you open bitch and make you eat your own organs."

Sarah had no time or energy to argue so ignored him and slowly spread herself so she was lying across his stomach barely missing the blade. He feebly punched her which under normal circumstances she would barely feel, but these were not those circumstances and each punch was like being hit by a hammer. But still she resisted. Her fingers barely able to open, instead curled into wicked, broken talons, with one hand she gripped his flaccid cock. An organ that had been inside her too many times against her will, every orifice possible. The kid could perhaps sense what was coming because he was getting more agitated, but she had hit him in the side of the head with a heavy ashtray, and it had done its job. He was unable to coordinate his actions properly. With her other hand, she gripped the rose stem as best she could.

Sarah's mother had always loved roses—it was an obligatory gift each birthday and also from Sarah's dad on Valentine's Day. But her mother had warned her from a very early age to always be careful while handling them and not just because of the sharp, deadly prickles. The stem was also covered in minute barbs, barely visible, but just as lethal if one were to rub a hand down it. It was these that Sarah was most interested in, the larger prickles having already been removed.

Unable to see what she was planning on doing, he must have been genuinely shocked and surprised to feel her hand on his cock. Whether he thought she was going to go down on him or not, she didn't know. She wouldn't put it past him, the sick, twisted individual. His groans that followed though were certainly not from pleasure. Slowly and carefully, she slid the rose stem into the urethra until it wouldn't go any further. About nine inches she guessed, so it must be prodding at his bladder or some other organ. She hoped it ruptured them. And then, she started raising and lowering the stem, up and down, slowly at first then faster, as if jerking him off. Droplets of blood dribbled from the tip of his cock, the stem now stained red. He screamed, frantically pummelling her with his fists, but Sarah held on, ramming that thing back down his cock, hoping she was tearing up the insides of it as they had done to her.

He shit himself, a stench foul and terrible, his shit smearing the backs of his legs that drummed repeatedly on the carpet. His eyes glazed over, all the whites showing as though possessed. His strength began to fade. She could hear the tearing of the flesh now as his screams died down. Little bits were stuck to the stem. Then, with the last of her own strength, she pushed the stem down as far as it would go until the petals sat proudly on the tip of his shrivelled, ripped dick, like a miniature vase.

Satisfied, she crawled off him but before she pulled herself to her feet to escape, she gripped him with both hands and squeezed and twisted as hard as she possibly could. Blood spurted from the tiny gaps around the stem. Last, she grabbed his cigarette lighter that so many times he had used on her and held the flame to the tip, so it melted and fused the hole closed.

"Let's see you fuck now, you piece of shit," she said and staggered off to look for help.

Chapter 2

Sarah Greenwood was in tears. She couldn't believe it. To the point she had to read the email several times before she fully understood what the words were telling her. As if written in a foreign language she had only the slightest grasp of. But there was no denying. The word *'congratulations'* was impossible to mistake for another.

Dear Sarah,

Congratulations are in order. After reading the rest of your novel between myself and the rest of the team, we have decided to go ahead and offer you a contract to publish your novel, Where Monsters Live. Please read the small print carefully, and...

Fuck the small print, she'd read that later. What was important was that first, short paragraph. Her first ever horror novel she'd spent almost a year writing, then rewriting until it was as perfect as it could possibly be, was to be published and in the bookstores soon. And she was still only sixteen.

It had to be impossible, they'd mistaken her for someone else, another Sarah. These things happened from time to time. The secretary having a bad day, not paying attention, and sending out emails to the wrong people. She read it for a fifth time, going over it carefully. Yes, that was her surname at the bottom, that was her email address, and that was definitely the title of her book.

"Oh my God, I'm gonna be a published fucking author," she whispered, barely capable of speaking, her tongue glued to the roof of her mouth. She got off the bed and stood up, looking at herself in the long mirror embedded into the wardrobe. Some people wrote books for years and never got published. They died of old age without getting published. Yet here she was, not even old enough to drink, vote, or drive; a child. Breasts barely visible through her pyjamas, still shorter than most girls in her class, not a freckle on her unblemished face. She ran her hands through shoulder-length permed, black hair, smiled at the bright, wide blue eyes that shone like stars, short stubby nose, thick, full lips. Right now, she felt as though she was floating, her already thin, frail body now so light she was going to fly to the moon. Her heart seemed to be preparing itself for the journey, revving inside her chest, ready for take-off. She had to suddenly sit back down on the bed before her legs gave way. She picked up her phone and read the email once more.

And then she was off. She screamed. Bounced up and down on the bed like a mischievous toddler. She couldn't stop screaming. She was sixteen years old, and her dreams had already come true. Sarah pinched herself to make sure it wasn't an actual dream. Her bedroom door burst open and frantic, worried parents entered.

"What? What's wrong?" asked her mother, Tina.

Her father, Eric, stood there, panic in his eyes as though he was witnessing some tragic event unfold, his police officer's uniform spotless as always.

"Mum, Dad, I did it! I did it!"

Her parents looked at each other, confused. They looked Sarah up and down as though she'd done something to herself.

"Slow down, Sarah and tell us!"

"My book! My novel that I wrote; they're gonna publish it! I just got the email! Look!"

She handed her mother her phone who took her time to read the email, Eric peering over her shoulder. It was comical to watch. Their jaws dropped simultaneously,

Am I a Monster?

while their lips slowly spread across their faces, their eyes widening. And then, frozen for a few seconds as they stared at their daughter, their lips started quivering, eyes now glassy. Her mother reacted first, almost dropping the phone on the floor and embraced Sarah so hard, she thought she might suffocate.

"Oh my God, Sarah! Congratulations. I don't believe it. I'm so proud of you. We both are."

"Well done, kid. Your mother's right—you've made us proud."

His Adam's apple was bobbing up and down. Sarah could tell he was struggling to contain himself. Eric was not a man to show his emotions very often. She'd only ever seen them once before.

"Now, show me it again!" exclaimed Tina. "How much are they paying you? When will it be released? I want a signed copy, you know. So will your grandmother. And your aunt. Oh, and don't forget your uncle, Timothy, and..."

Sarah made it to school with barely five minutes to spare.

She managed to contain her excitement until the morning's break without telling anyone, especially her best friend, Shelly. But when the bell rang, Shelly was quick to grab her arm.

"You've been smiling to yourself all morning. What happened? What's his name?"

"His name's, *Where Monsters Live*. My book, Shelly, I got the email this morning. They've accepted it; it's being published!"

Sarah then went through the same process as with her parents earlier that day. So far only Shelly and her parents knew about the book deal, but Sarah already had fifteen signed copies booked. The rest of the day was tedious, Sarah barely able to concentrate. She was already thinking of the sequel, dreaming of touring the local and national TV shows, proudly touting her new book. If she remembered correctly, she would receive around three thousand Euros upfront then fifty per cent royalties every six months with bonuses included. She saw herself in some of London's top fashion shops trying on clothes with Shelly they had only ever dreamed of. Then the movie rights would be sold, perhaps Brad Pitt cast as lead actor. She may get to meet him onset.

"Sarah! You gonna sit there all day and night? The bell just rang. You know, to go home?"

Sarah jumped, broken from her daydreaming by Shelly. She laughed and together they went to meet up with her small group of friends and give them the good news too. As they all sat huddled together on a bench outside school, everyone congratulating Sarah, she noticed a boy staring at her and smiling. Andrew Foreman, a boy she'd had a crush on for years but had never built up the courage to say anything to him. He was smiling and blushing a little too and she could tell he'd been eavesdropping, leaning against a tree pretending to scroll through his phone. Her other four girlfriends must have noticed also because they giggled and made their excuses, then left to go home. Andrew approached. Sarah's heart revved up again for the second time that day.

"Hey, Sarah, I hear congratulations are in order!"

"Thanks! Yeah, I'm super excited."

"So you should be! It's not every day one gets to be a published author. Or get to know one either. You deserve it. I'll need your autograph, of course."

Oh my God, my heart is gonna explode. This day cannot possibly get any better. Sarah knew when she was being flirted with. She hadn't had many boyfriends before and was generally quite shy and wary around

Am I a Monster?

boys, unlike Shelly who revelled in flirting with them. But she could see where this was heading.

"Thank you!" She tried to think of something else to say but her mind had shut off. When she was writing it was easy coming up with quick responses for her characters, but she was learning that in real life, it was another matter altogether. Especially when the boy she'd had a crush on for years had spoken more words to her in one minute than ever before.

He sat beside her. Other girls walked past, glared and nudged each other. Sarah wasn't the only one who had a crush on Andrew Foreman. There was a moment of awkward silence between them, Sarah's mind racing as she tried to think of something to say. Andrew broke the silence for them.

"So, I was thinking, you should, we should, you know, celebrate. How about I invite you out? We can grab a pizza or whatever you like—I'll pay. What do you say?"

If Sarah's heart had slipped into overdrive twice already that day, now it was going to explode and shatter her ribcage. She wasn't sure what was more exciting; the book contract or Andrew inviting her out on a date.

"Yeah, sure! Sounds cool! Thanks, I'd love to."

"Brilliant! How does tomorrow night sound, Friday?"

"Sounds good to me!"

"Done. See you tomorrow. Oh, and give me your number, I'll text you."

She did so and Andrew left. The journey home Sarah was convinced her feet hadn't touched the ground once. And when she phoned Shelly to tell her the exciting news, she burst out crying. It was theoretically impossible for Sarah to ever be as happy as she was on that short walk home.

Chapter 3

If Sarah had been nervous from the moment she submitted her novel to the publishers, wondering if she'd get an email back telling her it was crap and she should give up writing, it was nothing compared to the next day. She could barely keep her composure during lessons and a couple of times her teacher had to call her attention. She'd been staring out of the window instead of listening to the teacher and when he asked her the answer to a question she hadn't even heard, she'd blushed a deep red. Shelly told her so later.

And when she wasn't dreaming of marrying Andrew and having half a dozen kids taken care of by nannies while writing another New York Times bestseller, she was secretly glancing at the texts the boy was sending her every five minutes, some of which made her blush too. Andrew wasn't shy when it came to naughty memes, it seemed. It was possibly the slowest and most nerve-wrecking day in her life.

"Where you gonna go?" asked Shelly later that day.

"I dunno. Pizza maybe. He said I could choose, his way of saying congratulations on the book. Maybe a cocktail or two beforehand as well, he said."

"You're gonna get drunk as well! Wow, look at you go. All the other girls in school are super jealous, you know. Everyone knows he invited you out."

"Their problem, not mine. I did notice a few smirks and sneers directed at me though. But he asked me, not the other way around. What do they think I'm gonna do, say no?"

"Fuck 'em. Go for it. You deserve it for once. When was the last boyfriend you had?"

Am I a Monster?

"Mike, about six months ago. And what a prick he turned out to be."

"See! So things are changing for you. For the better. I wish I could swap Danny for Andrew. Wanna swap?"

"Eww, no way. You can keep him. Danny's not my type anyway."

"You don't have a type, Sarah. Anyway, you gonna do anything with him, like afterwards?" Shelly winked.

"On a first date? Yeah, sure. Then they'll be calling me something completely different at school. That'll be fun."

Sarah had no intentions of doing anything with Andrew at all. She knew Shelly wasn't a virgin, as neither was Sarah, but there was a big difference between her view on such matters and Shelly's. Once Shelly got a couple of margaritas inside her, she was often more than happy to have plenty of other things inside her as well.

Sarah found herself avoiding Andrew throughout the day, too embarrassed to be near him in case she blushed or got tongue-tied. Not to mention all the other girls spying on them. When she saw him heading in her direction, she either darted into the toilets or turned around and bolted the other way. She'd worry about matters later when they were together and alone. But she did promise Shelly that she'd text her to make sure everything was okay. On one occasion Shelly had gone out with another boy, who'd got drunk then practically raped her before she managed to escape. That wasn't going to happen with Sarah.

When she got home, she had a bath and began the process of getting dressed and applying makeup.

"Need any help?" asked her mother.

"Nah, I'm good."

She had gone for a more sensible look, wearing jeans

which admittedly clung to her so much it was as if they'd been painted on and a pink top that only hinted at what was below. Sarah didn't have very big breasts anyway and was conscious of the fact, especially when comparing herself to Shelly, who appeared to have two fully inflated balloons under her top. But if Andrew was only after one thing anyway, he was out of luck.

"How do I look?"

"Wonderful. But really, Sarah, aren't those jeans a little tight? Couldn't you wear something a little…baggier? You know what boys are like at that age. They only think of one thing."

"Andrew's different, Mum. Besides, we're just gonna share a pizza and that's it. I'll be home by twelve."

"Well, that's what they all say, at first. Trying to be all polite and nice. If he so much as tries or says anything, you call me. Or even better, your father. He's on the night shift tonight, so he'll be patrolling."

"Will do, Mum."

Is this where the legendary talk was about to happen? Again? Sarah was sixteen but her mother seemed to think she was stuck in a perpetual age of thirteen and needed to be taught and reminded of life's little mysteries constantly. Instead, for the third time in two days, Sarah was about to be reduced to a blubbering mess.

"Oh, I was going to wait until your father was here, but I just couldn't. We, umm, have a little surprise. As congratulations for your book being published."

Sarah stopped applying makeup in the mirror and turned to face her mother. "What have you gone and done now?"

"Well, it's cold now, being March and all that and it's cold pretty much everywhere too, so we booked a flight for April, when apparently it starts getting a little

Am I a Monster?

warmer. Much warmer than here anyway, but—"

"Where?!"

"Well, you always said you wanted to go to Barcelona, so we booked a week there, for April. To celebrate and—"

Sarah screamed.

Then hugged her mother as tightly as she'd been hugged the day before. She'd always wanted to go to Barcelona. Especially after seeing the architecture by Gaudi, the Sagrada Familia being top of her list. When she read that he died after being run over by a tram, it turned him into a mythical figure for her and she had to visit one day his beautiful creations. Plus, The Ramblas, the sea, try paella, sangria, everything. And now they were going.

"I thought you'd be pleased!"

"Oh my God, Mum, thank you so much! I was thinking of using some of the money from the book to go there on a long weekend."

"Well, now you can save your money for something else."

When Sarah arrived at the bar she'd agreed to meet Andrew at, she was still texting back and forth with Shelly, telling her about the trip to Barcelona. Andrew was sat at the bar sipping a Coca Cola. Her heart shrivelled again—this was way too much excitement for one lifetime.

"Hey, Andrew. Been waiting long?"

"Nah, just got here. You okay?"

She told him about the trip. He congratulated her, sounding genuine, his smile and eyes warm. Her mother's surprise killed off any chance of awkward beginnings too. Sarah immediately started giving Andrew a history of Gaudi, the places she wanted to visit in Barcelona, and this inevitably led to a discussion on all the places they'd visited before and would like to go to one day. It was as if they'd been friends for life. Both looked older than sixteen so when they ordered margaritas, the barman didn't ask for ID. They'd drunk two before Andrew turned to her and asked her a question that came out of nowhere and she hadn't been prepared for.

"So, you wanna come back to my place for another drink? My older brother has a spare flat that's empty. He works and pretty much lives in London, so barely uses it. I often stay there when I wanna throw a party or somethin'."

The two drinks had gone to her head, so her immediate thought was yes, she did want to go, but the sensible part of her that was still awake and functional somewhere deep inside questioned whether it was a good idea or not. But they'd been chatting for over two hours, and Andrew hadn't made a single suggestive comment to her or touched her. If anything, it had been her that touched him, occasionally grabbing his arm when wanting to tell him something exciting about herself or discuss her book. They might have been brother and sister should anyone watch them. And besides, he was one of the most popular kids at school—he wouldn't be so stupid as to ruin his reputation.

"Okay, cool!" she said. But just in case, she texted Shelly to let her know where she was going.

Andrew paid the bill and together they left to go to Andrew's flat.

Am I a Monster?

Chapter 4

"Two doctors are having a drink in a bar. They've never met but start chatting. So what do you do? asks one. I'm a doctor, the other replies. Oh, nice, says the other, so am I. How's it going? Wonderful, he says. Plenty of patients, can't complain. How about you?

"Ah, man, I'm in trouble. One of my patients has filed a complaint against me, I may lose my license. I was caught having sex with a patient.

"C'mon, that's not such a big deal. We've all been through that. You'll be fine, don't worry."

"Yeah, but I'm a vet."

There was an ominous moment of silence while Sarah replayed the joke in her head then she got it. She burst out laughing. Andrew breathed a sigh of relief and laughed with her.

"Brilliant," she said between chuckles. "A vet!"

She sat on his sofa nursing a beer, which she didn't really like, but he had nothing else except strong liquor. Those two margaritas had really gone to her head, so better not push it, she reasoned, and risk making a fool of herself. If she threw up on his sofa and hands started probing where they shouldn't she'd die of shame. Fortunately, he wasn't sitting right next to her but across from her on a chair which made her feel more comfortable. She appreciated that from him. It was as if he sensed that she needed or preferred a little space between them; other boys would have been slavering at the mouth, and all over her by now.

What she didn't like so much and was trying to keep an eye on was how much he was drinking himself. Like a hardened alcoholic, he had already knocked back two

Jack Daniels and Coke. His face was red and flushed, like his eyeballs. Starting to slur his words making it hard to understand him. It was starting to make her a little uncomfortable this fact alone—boys and people in general did stupid things when drunk. She wondered if she should make an excuse and leave, but first, she couldn't think of a decent excuse, tomorrow being Saturday, so she had no reason to get up early, and she'd only been here an hour. It wasn't even ten yet.

He'd think she wasn't interested which was far from the truth. He might be popular in school with the girls, but this didn't necessarily mean he was confident around them. Maybe he was drinking so much now because it was a first date and he was nervous. Andrew was chatting away, getting his words mixed up while he told joke after joke, fumbling with his hands and constantly shifting on his seat. Sarah could barely get a word in. She had so many things she wanted to chat about but now it all seemed like a waste of time. Tomorrow, he probably wouldn't remember half of it. Maybe she could tell him she had to get up early tomorrow, that she had a meeting with someone who was going to go through the book contract with her and it was important. Yeah, that might work. Over the weekend they could agree to meet again and Andrew would no doubt apologise profusely for drinking too much but he had been so nervous and he really liked Sarah and didn't want to screw things up and…

He rose and came and sat beside her, a smirk on his face she didn't like at all.

Andrew staggered when he approached her, his empty glass swinging dangerously in his hand.

"I really like you, Sarah. Like, really, really. Always did but never dare say anythin'. You like me too, don't ya?"

Am I a Monster?

"Yes, I do, Andrew, but I think you've had too much to drink, and I really need to get going anyway. I have an important mee—"

She never got to finish her excuse, because his lips were now on hers. His tongue poked out like a curious worm. She tried to push him away, but he dropped his glass which smashed on the tiled floor and then his arms were around her, not so much embracing her as clutching her in a bearhug. She could barely breathe. Sarah pulled her head away from him so she could talk.

"Andrew, stop. You're hurting me. I really need to go, plea—"

But again, he wouldn't let her finish. His lips smacked against hers, his breath reeking of alcohol, his tongue probing, running over her cheek rather than into her mouth as he searched for a way in. Then, she felt his hand on her thigh, snaking its way up and before she could react, his hand was between her legs. She was glad she'd decided to wear jeans because he was fumbling with the buttons trying to undo them as she gripped his hand and attempted to push him off.

Finally, she managed to create a little space between them.

"Andrew, stop now! I don't like it. You're drunk. I need to get home. Get off me."

She pushed him, a little harder than she intended but he was scaring her. He fell onto the floor and lay there sprawled over the shards from his broken glass. He looked shocked. He also looked extremely pissed, glaring at her, a sneer breaking across his features, blood dripping from his hand he wasn't even aware of.

"Andrew, I…I'm sorry, I didn't mean to push you to the floor, but you were hurting me. I need to go. Sorry."

She stood up, but he gripped her ankle and stopped her from leaving. "You bitch. Who the fuck do ya think you are? Fuckin' published author, do what you want, is that it? Better than everyone else?"

"Andrew, you're drunk. Just…I'll text you tomorrow. Let me go now."

He tugged her, almost causing her to trip. She had no choice but to use her free foot to step on his wrist. A crunching sound followed as his hand was pressed down hard on the shards. Blood dripped everywhere, pieces of glass embedded in his hand. He seemed completely unaware.

"Fuckin' bitch, you're gonna pay for this, you fuckin' snob. No one fuckin' pushes me."

Her foot pressing down harder, he was forced to let her go. He tried to grab her again and only then did he realise his hands were covered in blood. He pulled out one long shard and threw it at her face. Without wasting more time, and sobbing uncontrollably, Sarah ran from the flat, his screams and insults ringing in her ears even as she ran onto the cold street. She didn't stop running or crying until she reached the safety of her own home.

Am I a Monster?

Chapter 5

Sarah's dreams had somehow, through absolutely no fault of her own, become a nightmare. In her fantasy world, relived endless number of times already in the bubble she'd created in her mind, she would be living in a mansion somewhere in the south of England. Writing the next best-seller while Andrew doted over her, the roles reversed—she the one earning all the hard cash while Andrew kept himself amused with their children, perhaps running his own business. Or a footballer even, playing for one of the top teams in England, body fit and lean, but only having eyes for her. Now though, that bubble had popped and in spectacular fashion.

The simple fact that she was home before eleven would have told her mother everything she needed to know. A first date and home early? There could only be one reason for that. Sarah had stopped to catch her breath and dry her eyes before entering but it wouldn't have made any difference, either. She opened the front door, trying to be quiet so her mother didn't hear then rushed upstairs and locked herself in her room, but her mother had heard the door open and come looking. Being married to a policeman instinctively instilled caution and worry in her, too many horror tales heard to ignore unexpected noises. But her mother didn't have to say anything. Sarah guessed her face was puffy from crying, eyes bloodshot, home early—enough said. She did ask her if she was okay, but Sarah just muttered some unintelligible response and ran upstairs. Her mother no doubt knew not to interfere unless it was necessary to do so.

Sarah had thrown herself onto her bed, replayed every

moment, every insult, every grope from Andrew over and over, sobbing again as she did so. She thought of texting Shelly to tell her what happened, she tried to convince herself that this was not who Andrew really was; it was a mistake, he'd fucked up and it would never happen again. But what if it did? She was too tired, too distraught to tell Shelly anyway, also telling herself that Shelly would laugh at her, not understanding the terror she had been through, thinking Andrew was going to rape her there and then. Shelly would laugh and say she should have taken advantage of the situation—dozens of girls would beg to fuck Andrew. What was wrong with her? Shelly would never understand the moment of dread or repulsion as he practically squeezed the life out of her, his breath reeling of whisky, hands fumbling around her jeans like a desperate perv. Tongue prodding like an alien probe. When the kid had tried to rape Shelly, she had kicked him in the balls then left him there while she taunted and spat at him. Shelly found it hilarious the kid had the audacity to try and rape her.

And yet, another part of her was in denial. It had been her fault. She had been flirting with him, laughing a little too hard at his jokes. Hadn't her own mother told her that her jeans were too tight, too provocative? What did she expect then from a drunken teen? Without realising Sarah had been leading him along, just waiting for him to come and sit next to her and start groping. If he hadn't it would not have been normal either. People would think he was gay and if that got out, he'd never hear the end of it. So really, he had only been doing what was expected of him and things just got a little out of hand. If someone pushed her on the floor, causing her to inadvertently cut her hands to shreds on the broken glass, yeah, she'd be throwing a few insults around too.

But still, none of that took away the immense pain and

Am I a Monster?

sense of betrayal she'd felt. She had been so looking forward to their date, utterly convinced he wouldn't do anything stupid because he just didn't seem that kind of guy. He had a pretty good reputation among the kids at school as being friendly with everyone; Sarah couldn't even remember him getting into a fight, let alone trying to force himself on another girl. Only one time, maybe, when some other kid had been looking just a little too long at his then girlfriend. Andrew had asked him what the fuck he was doing, a push and shove had ensued and Andrew had punched him in the nose, shattering it instantly. He'd had to be pulled away from the other kid too, screaming and hurling insults at him, that he was an arsehole and he was going to kill him. Just like an hour ago…

Sarah fell asleep fantasising about mansions and nannies and bestsellers and football hero husbands.

When she awoke the next morning, it took a few seconds to remember the events of the previous night. What seemed like a millisecond of happiness, a smile on her face as had been the case since receiving the email, was bitterly snatched from her as Andrew's drunken sneer popped into her memory bank. The threats and insults bounced around inside her head, around the room as though brought back to life again. Her body sagged, eyes glazed and clouded with tears as the recollection of everything that had happened threatened to overwhelm her with sadness. Now that she had had time to sleep on it, she once more tried to find light and reason in a dark world, looking for justifications from the boy when deep down she knew there were none.

She picked up her phone and glanced at the time—almost ten in the morning. She'd slept nearly twelve hours. Not necessarily a record breaker but close. Andrew would be awake now she assumed; what would be going through his mind? She checked her messages. She wasn't sure if she was glad or not, maybe she should put it down to a learning experience and forget about Andrew altogether, but when she saw the texts from Andrew, her reaction was the opposite. She sat up and read through all seven of them, all pretty much saying the same thing:

Sarah, I'm so sorry. Please forgive me. Was nervous, got drunk. Won't happen again. I swear. Please tell me you'll see me again.

It ended with a series of heart emojis which nearly broke her own heart. What was she to do? If she told her mum what happened, she'd be shocked and not only tell her to stay the hell away from him, but she'd probably warn her dad as well. And that would definitely be the end of that. He was far too protective of her as it was. Sarah was easy to forgive mistakes and perfectly understood Andrew had drunken too much due to nerves—she'd almost done the same herself, but he'd crossed a line. It hadn't just been a quick fumble or a suggestion they take things further; if she'd let him, he would have pulled her jeans off there and then. And she didn't think just telling him no would have had much effect either.

She should speak with Shelly. In person. Once she'd described just how far Andrew had gone, she wouldn't find it so funny anymore. Shelly had far more experience with boys than she did, so would know what to do, what to say. And her response would probably be to stay away as well, fuck him, he was dangerous. But Sarah didn't want to.

Surely, in the cold light of day, no alcohol present, he could explain his actions, they could spend the day together and she could get to know the real Andrew. After that, she could make a decision. It was only fair

Am I a Monster?

she let him explain himself.

Sarah responded to his texts saying that if he liked they could meet after lunch. For coffee. Within seconds he replied.

Thank you so much, Sarah. I promise I won't touch a drop of alcohol this time!

Shelly had been bugging her with texts all morning too, wanting to know how it went, what they had done, how big he was. That was all she ever thought about, the little slut. Sarah told her so and she'd have to wait to hear all the juicy details—they were meeting again after lunch, she'd let her know.

Sarah arrived at the cosy, little bar at three to find Andrew sitting at a table, his back to her. He had a coffee beside him, so it looked like he was sticking to his word. A good sign.

"Hey, Andrew."

He jumped upon hearing her and spun around. There was a smile on his face which quickly disappeared, to be replaced by a look of shame. "Sarah, thanks for coming. I didn't think you would. Look, I just want to say before anything else, I feel like a total arsehole. That was not me at all. Honestly, I don't know what I was thinking. I'll never touch alcohol again. I promise."

She said nothing and sat on the opposite chair across the table from him. Her heart was torn; on the one hand she really wanted to forgive him, but on the other; a vision returned of the insults, the sneer on his face, look of hate, his hand fumbling with her jeans. He did look so sincere though, and were they tears brewing in his eyes?

"So, do you forgive me? Can we…carry on seeing each other? I promise I won't tell no more naughty vet jokes either!"

That brought a chuckle from her. She ordered a coffee while she thought about it. It didn't take long. "Okay, but next time, no booze and keep your hands to yourself!"

The beaming smile on Andrew's face was so big and wide, it made her chuckle again. As if nothing had happened the night before, they resumed telling each other their dreams and hopes, discussing music, TV series they enjoyed on Netflix, other kids and teachers at school. It was almost two hours later when Andrew suggested they go back to his older brother's flat. He wanted to show her some things on his laptop, a short story he'd written himself a year ago and wanted her advice. For a brief moment, doubt wriggled its way through her body. She really didn't want to go back to that place and relive the events of last night, but if she was to give him a second chance, and considering he virtually lived at the flat alone nowadays she couldn't put it off forever. She agreed.

Feeling slightly hesitant, she stepped inside and was immediately assaulted by an avalanche of sensations and flashbacks, none of them good. She swayed on her feet, grit her teeth and quickly sat down. But at the table not on the sofa. She thought she could still smell the pungent odour of his sweat and the alcohol on his breath and instinctively closed her legs tight.

"You okay?" he asked.

"Yeah, fine! So what's this short story of yours? I'm eager to read it!"

She wasn't, but anything to avoid answering his question.

"Ah, yeah! Come and have a look at this. You don't mind horror, right? It's not gory or anything, but I hope it's pretty creepy."

He wandered off to another room, which she assumed was an office or writing area. She also assumed she was meant to follow behind him, so she slowly and carefully pulled herself to her feet, her legs still slightly unstable

Am I a Monster?

and headed after him. He was chatting about his story, but she couldn't quite hear what he was saying now—it was a large flat. She entered the room and saw it was a bedroom but there was indeed a desk with a laptop on it, that he was turning on. That momentary twitch of unease dissipated after seeing first the bed, then the laptop. For a moment, she wondered if…

"See, what do you think? It's not very long, but I'd like to write more if this one's any good. Here."

He turned the laptop so she was looking at the screen. Sarah approached it and bent over to read his story.

And suddenly found herself lying on the floor, her head as if it had been cracked open with a hammer. The room was spinning and blurry and when she tried to push herself to her feet, her brain refused to comply with the demand. She rose a few inches then collapsed again. Sarah opened her mouth to ask for help, she must have slipped or something but she found it impossible to speak either, as if suddenly rendered mute. Only a groan came instead.

She was vaguely aware of something warm and wet underneath her head, a coppery smell to it she thought she might recognise. And then, as if she'd been magically scooped up by angels, she found herself rising effortlessly and was dropped onto the soft bed. Sarah tried to say thank you to Andrew for helping her get up but found it impossible to say the words. She looked up at him, a blurred outline, like a ghost, but was conscious enough to notice he wasn't doing anything to help her, just standing there, looking down at her. Sarah reached out an arm to grab him, beg for help, but he swiped it away as though some troublesome fly. He was saying something to her, but she had no idea what—only a distant humming in her ears was all she heard.

After a few minutes or what might have been hours—

she had no concept of time anymore—she was then aware of Andrew helping her. She didn't know what she had done to herself, but he was tugging at her clothes. Maybe she'd broken her leg or something as well and it was bleeding badly because he was pulling off her jeans. But then she saw rather than felt as her underwear was removed when Andrew tore it off and threw it away. She raised her head to see what she'd done to herself, her head screaming in protest and tried to ask him what he was doing, because she couldn't see any blood on her legs at all and she was now completely naked below the waist.

And then, her jumbled mind fit the pieces together for her.

Especially when she saw him pulling his own jeans off. She blinked rapidly, trying to regain her vision and tried to sit up. This was a nightmare. She wasn't awake but had fallen asleep and the memories of last night had come for her again, but the incessant throbbing at the back of her head as if she was being stabbed repeatedly there, told her the real story. It was a nightmare all right, but one she was living in flesh and blood.

The shock of seeing what he was doing must have helped her brain regain some of its functions because now the feelings in her arms and legs was returning. The fogginess from her vision slowly cleared and now she could understand what Andrew was saying.

"…bitch is ever gonna turn me down and make me out to look an idiot. Last time someone pushed me over, I kicked the fuckin' shit outta him. Think you're fuckin' clever with your stupid book, I'm gonna show you what's clever."

He was naked now too, his cock hard and throbbing. For reasons she would never understand she thought of Shelly and how she'd wish she was here with Andrew

Am I a Monster?

instead—his was the kind of thing she'd seen on porn sites and had giggled and wowed over with her friend. The strength slowly returned to her arms and legs, her brain finally coordinating her actions with something resembling logic. She lashed out at him, still weak, which he dodged easily. She pushed herself up so she could get off the bed and run, but another bolt of lightning struck her on the back of the head. Then what felt like another when his fist connected with her jaw and she collapsed again.

Sarah tried to scream. There was no way she was walking or running out of here with a mild concussion, but her throat was too dry, devoid of any saliva and all that came out was a breathless groan.

"Fuck you think you're goin', huh? You ain't going anywhere bitch, for a long time."

"Please," she squeaked. "Sorry, I'm so—"

But Andrew wasn't listening. He was standing beside her now, his cock inches from her face. She could smell the tang of his sweat there as if he hadn't showered in days. Then she felt herself being dragged higher up the bed, her arms above her head. She writhed and struggled, tried to twist her way out of his grasp, but she was too weak and him too strong. Something brought her wrists together, something tight that instantly cut the circulation and when she tried to pull away, her arms were stuck fast. He'd tied her to the bed. Now, she was at the mercy of a deranged teen whose pride had taken a serious knock. Never would she have expected him to go through with what was obviously coming. He was the school heartthrob, the kid all the girls wanted to be with. And now he was going to rape her?

"Open your fuckin' legs. You're gettin' what you deserve. I bet you told your friends about kickin' me and they're all fuckin' laughin' behind my back. Well, I'm the one doin' the laughin' now, ain't I?"

Sarah entered full-on panic mode. She'd recovered her senses and strength once more and lashed out at him with both feet, hoping to catch him in the jaw or the balls. If she could injure him there in the balls, it might give her time to scream or find a way out of this. But Andrew was too fast for her and probably expecting it. He roughly grabbed an ankle and tied it to the side of the bed, then the other, splitting her legs apart. It occurred to her that she hadn't seen him fetch any rope so it must have been hidden beneath the bed. That meant he was either into kinky sex with girls or he had been planning this. She guessed the latter option was the more likely. And also the scariest.

She opened her mouth to scream but when she did so, her sock was shoved inside. A strip of duct tape was then put across her lips. Sarah thrashed as hard and as much as she possibly could. If he was going to fuck her, she wasn't going to make it easy or pleasant for him. Even so, when he climbed onto the bed and forced his cock inside her, there was very little she could do stop him. He rammed her hard causing her head to bang against the headboard sending more shockwaves through her brain and down her back.

"Nice, tight little pussy, you got there, bitch. Nice and wet too. See, I knew you were a little slut, been waiting for it all along, wasn't ya?"

Her vagina was on fire. The kid she'd lost her virginity too had been so careful and gentle with her, but now it was as if Andrew had shoved a red hot fire poker inside her, melting the walls of her vagina and her intestines. And the more she struggled, the more he seemed to be enjoying it, drooling at the mouth, grinning an insane grin, sweating profusely. He spat in her face, a big, thick blob of saliva that trickled down her cheek.

Am I a Monster?

The assault seemed to go on forever. Sarah tried to block him out by thinking of her novel, returning to that fantasy world again where she lived in a mansion, but this time there was no football hero husband by her side, only her and her laptop. She imagined awards dotted around the room, her books lining her shelves. But every time she opened her eyes, a monster loomed over her, and the fantasy world was gone.

Finally, he came, right inside her, and she wanted to throw up, knowing no amount of scrubbing was going to take away the feeling of filth. But it was done. Now, he would threaten her with her life if she said anything, then untie her and let her go. That was all she wanted right now, but instead, Andrew's words caused utter terror to freeze her muscles.

"Good fuck, bitch. I'll be back again tonight for another. Bring the boys too. Might as well make yourself comfortable—you're here for a long time."

And with that, Andrew got dressed and headed out.

Chapter 6

Andrew was happy with himself as he headed off to his friend's house. Nothing like a good fuck to clear one's mind. He'd been wanting to fuck Sarah for ages too. It should have happened the other night, but yes, he had to admit he'd had too much to drink. He'd been nervous, not wanting to fuck it up. Well, he certainly did that. But for Sarah to then go and push him onto the floor, causing him to cut his palms to shreds, no one did that and got away with it. She'd probably ran home and told all her friends about it and they'd been laughing behind his back since. Yet another humiliating situation he'd been put in.

And he was sick of it. This time, he was going to make sure no one ever did that to him again. She was going to pay and big time, not just for what she did but for what they all did. Okay, it wasn't meant to go that far, his plan had been to fuck her, tell her that if she ever told anyone, he'd come for her and her family, but things had got a little out of control. Thinking things through properly was not one of Andrew's strong points. It may have been the way Sarah had tried to struggle, kick him in the balls, hurt him again, that did it, or it may have been years of neglect and a low self-esteem which had finally erupted, chaos raining down on Sarah that triggered his actions earlier. Regardless, it was too late to back down now. Not that he wanted to anyway. Now, for once in his shitty, pathetic life he was in control. He was the one dictating order, deciding how events should unfold, no one else. Certainly, not his father who he hadn't seen in years—and thank fuck for that—or his stupid mother who only seemed to have time and love for the bottle.

Am I a Monster?

Maybe he was just being over-sensitive. Millions of kids around the world came from dysfunctional families, regularly abused, starved, or just unloved, but it still didn't make his life any easier. It was hard work playing the cool kid at school when all he wanted was to just curl up and die most of the time. Not have to play a role so other kids and the girls liked him, but actually liked him for who he was inside. And what happens? Just when he thought he might have found that someone in Sarah, she goes all apeshit on him and kicks him to the floor like he was a piece of shit. Just how everyone else treated him.

But not anymore.

Andrew wasn't an egoist either. He was certainly going to share his new toy with his friends. He knew he could trust them to keep their mouths shut—they wanted some excitement in their lives as much as he did. And besides, now that he really thought about it, nothing would stop Sarah from running to the police the minute he let her go, and there was no way he was going to juvenile and from there, prison. He'd been living in a prison his whole life; to spend the next ten years locked up in a literal one was not going to happen.

They'd surely treat him worse than his own father had. Beating him with his belt, telling him what a worthless, useless piece of shit he was, an unwanted kid. An accident. Making him drink from the toilet bowel when his father was drunk, the water in the toilet dirty, unflushed. His mother laughing while he did it. She still laughed at him now. Or cackling was maybe a better word behind thick cigarette smoke. Taunting him about what a tiny little dick he had and no girl was ever going to want to suck that. To this day he couldn't stand the sight of an unflushed toilet. Anytime someone used his and they forgot to flush he would go into a rage, threatening to drown them in the dirty water if they ever forgot again.

She once offered—while shitfaced drunk—to do it as a birthday present. She even went so far as to start unzipping his trousers, while his father smirked and watched. Such had been his embarrassment, he ran to his bedroom and pushed his bed against the door so she couldn't get in. And she'd tried to do just that. Another year on his fourteenth birthday, he'd woken in the middle of the night to find his mother in his bed next to him, completely naked and fondling him. Even worse was that he'd got a hard-on from it, until he realised who it was. She told him that no one would need to know, it was only sex, after all; what did it matter who one did it with? That night, he locked himself in the bathroom, refusing to come out. Six months later he finally lost his virginity with a girl from school, but it had almost been a disaster. He kept seeing his mother's face beneath him instead of the girl's.

Considering that since his father left when Andrew was ten, his mother regularly brought men back to the house, sometimes two at a time, why she felt the need to try and seduce him as well, he didn't know. At the time he had thought it strange she had so many different boyfriends until a few years later when he saw the transactions taking place and now knew how she could afford to pay the bills. She certainly wasn't working during the day while he was at school. And now, six years later, she was still doing it.

Andrew's brother, Karl, two years older, had known what was going on but instead of helping him had ran at the first opportunity. He'd been the apple of his parent's eyes, a first born, a child they actually wanted. And when it was discovered his intelligence was way above the norm they almost pissed themselves with excitement, thinking that Karl would get some high-flying job and

Am I a Monster?

put an end to their shitty state of existence. But they forgot that Karl wasn't stupid. He took his exams and six months later was living abroad, something to do with tech in Silicon Valley. He bought the flat where Andrew spent most of his time these days and left Andrew with the key. That had been Karl's way of helping his little brother. Not even their mother knew the flat existed. But Andrew hadn't spoken with his brother since then. He'd given up on his brother too—abandoned him to his fate.

So really, he guessed it wasn't a surprise that he had lost his patience with Sarah and had got carried away with her. In a way she had been taunting him as his mother did, leading him on, begging for it when one thought about it. And so, he had given her what she wanted—a good fuck. That what's they all want really, he told himself. Even his own mother. But Sarah was going to get a lot more than that. She was going to pay for every whipping, every slap, every mouthful of dirty, toilet water, every cigarette burn on his arms and face he'd received over the years. It was time to take control of things for once in his miserable life so that no one ever laughed or hurt him again. Maybe he'd even do the same to his mother one of these days—let the boys fuck her to death.

Fuck 'em all.

Andrew reached his friend's house where everyone hung out, drinking beer and smoking dope and knocked on the door. His friends were the same age as he was, in their last year of school but they had all given up on any expectations of a career a long time ago. They were his gang, his best friends. True friends. And he had the perfect present to give to them. If Sarah ever made it out of this, she'd want to become a nun, never have a man between her legs for the rest of her life.

Chapter 7

Sarah's parents managed to restrain themselves until ten that night. It was a Saturday and she was sixteen which meant they knew in their hearts they had to give Sarah a bit of leeway, let her breathe, give her some time, but that she hadn't answered her phone all evening was something she had never done. Kids nowadays were glued to their phones—she would never not reply to a simple text asking if she was coming home for supper. And the image that kept coming back to Tina as she nervously fiddled with her hands, fidgeting on the sofa, checking her phone every two minutes, was Sarah rushing home the night before. She knew that look well; it was one of having been through some horrible experience, not wanting one's parents to see she'd been crying. Tina might be forty-three, but she remembered her experiences with boys as a teen like it was yesterday. The boys who couldn't keep their hands to themselves, wanting to burrow a little deeper, touch where they weren't supposed to. And not all boys were so accepting when the girl said no. Tina knew, in her heart, that something very similar had happened to her daughter. Then the next day, this morning, she says she's off to see him again, and now where was she?

Tina didn't like this at all.

And then there was the question of whether to say anything to Eric yet. He was out on patrol, working the night shift as always. He'd drilled into them both on numerous occasions that at the slightest indication of trouble, regardless of who or what it was, to phone him. He knew better than anyone the monsters that lived on earth. And a sixteen-year-old girl was often a favourite

Am I a Monster?

victim. At the same time though, a false alarm, and he was prone to losing his temper, saying he had more important things to do than deal with a silly argument between mother and daughter. Not that it happened very often but Tina still found it incredibly hard to accept Sarah wasn't her little girl anymore—she was practically an adult who needed to figure things out for herself.

So, to phone Eric or not?

Tina picked up her phone and rang Sarah's number yet again. Now, it went straight to voicemail, even worse. Sarah didn't have a huge number of friends but the few she did have were good, faithful friends, that often came over and they all sat in Sarah's room discussing whatever teenage girls talked about. Shelly was her best friend and being Saturday night, maybe Sarah was with her, they'd gotten to chatting and Sarah had simply forgot to inform her mother. It happened. She'd done it herself at the same age, coming home and subjected to the wrath of worried parents. But there hadn't been mobile phones back then; now, all it took was a few seconds to text a message. So why hadn't Sarah done so? If only she had Shelly's number too, or even knew where she lived. Anything before making the inevitable call to Eric.

Tina racked her brains trying to think where Sarah might be or where any of her friends lived. Bradwell was a small village, here on the east coast of England, but it might as well have been a city when it came to knowing where her daughter may be. This boy, what had his name been? Andrew, was it? She'd never heard of him before, and Sarah had never brought any boys home with her; having a father who was a cop was usually enough deterrent to any boys who wanted Sarah to be their girlfriend. Maybe Sarah was lying injured somewhere, this Andrew having tried his luck with her, too much to drink perhaps, and he'd lost control. Happened all the time. Just down the road was Northgate Hospital for the Criminally Insane like an ominous shadow hovering above her, reminding her constantly that there were men who did such things and far, far worse. Fingers of terror were already prodding at Tina with the mere thought something bad may have happened.

She checked her watch. Ten-thirty now. This was now unprecedented, weekend or not. She hadn't heard from Sarah since midday.

"Damn you, Sarah. You're gonna make me do it, aren't you?"

She stared at her phone, willing it to ring or ping, a message from Sarah. But her phone was ignoring her as was her reasoning and belief that everything was fine.

She dialled Eric's number.

"What do you mean you haven't heard from her all day? And you're telling me *now*?"

"Well, I figured that it being Saturday, with this friend of hers they probably didn't realise what the time was but she's not answering my texts and now it's going straight to voicemail. I didn't want to worry you for nothing."

"Fuck. Okay, let's keep calm. Who was she with?"

"A boy from school. Andrew something."

"A *boy*? Christ. How long has she known him? Been seeing him?"

"Well, they go to the same school so she must have known him a while. As for seeing him, they went out last night. They've met up again today."

"And I don't suppose you have a surname for this kid? Let alone where he lives?"

The tears started rolling down her face. She imagined those terrible, haunting moments on the true crime documentaries she liked to watch where the parents were

Am I a Monster?

faced with a barrage of questions by detectives. Imaging how they must feel having to try and recall every little detail so they could track their missing kids. She saw herself at the press conference, clinging to Eric's arm as she begged for information, for someone to please come forward. That Sarah was going to be a published author at the tender age of sixteen and was so excited, so there was no way she would have run off. The flashes from the journalist's cameras, hers and Sarah's face on every newspaper throughout the country. Maybe on Unsolved Crimes in a few years. That brought a fresh batch of tears.

"No, I don't. I've been trying to think where her friends live, but I don't know!"

"Okay, calm down. I'll call dispatch, try and get the information. In fact, fuck it, I'm nearby, I'll go myself. If she does come home or phone, tell me immediately. I'll let you know as soon as I know anything myself."

Eric hung up, leaving Tina feeling scared, helpless and hopeless. She knew, as only mothers can truly know, that something was terribly wrong. Wanting to do something, start searching for her, but knowing she had to be here in case her daughter came home, she decided to keep herself busy. A cup of tea for her nerves then find something to watch on Netflix. Anything except true crime documentaries.

###

Eric always wondered if the day would come. He'd seen so much horror on the streets it seemed inevitable that one day it would follow him home like a faithful pet, attach itself to him to involucrate his beloved daughter. Both he and Tina had considered themselves so fortunate and lucky to have a responsible daughter, especially given the sad and often tragic stories he heard and saw on an almost daily basis. Kids abandoned by their parents, who turn to drugs and alcohol at such an early age. Maybe running away from home, girls prostituting themselves in hopes of saving money for a better future. Only last month, he had been called to a domestic where a fourteen-year-old girl had been beaten by her drunken father. The girl had required stitches on her forehead but despite the injuries sustained neither the girl nor her mother wanted to press charges. As with most similar cases, he assumed it was because they were afraid of the repercussions of doing so. Eric had had a quiet word with the man, letting him know he was watching and that if he ever touched his wife or daughter again, him and his colleagues may take matters into their own hands. The man, half drunk, smiled and said nothing. The man's wife was admitted to hospital just three days later with a broken arm and several contusions. One of Eric's colleagues 'found' ten grams of cocaine on the man and he was subsequently arrested. Sometimes justice came from other avenues.

But now, what he had hoped and prayed would never happen, it seemed had happened. This time, it was his life being exposed to horrors seen and unseen. If this Andrew kid had done anything, *anything*, to his baby girl, it wouldn't be a few grams of cocaine found in his pockets. It would be the kid's head instead.

He'd often thought about returning to life at the Serious Crimes Department, but he wasn't sure he could cope with that again. He'd gone back to being a uniformed officer six years ago and had seen enough without making it even worse. The added stress and longer hours. For what? To spend his evenings and days chasing down the kind of people where even Northgate was too good for them. He'd rather spend it with his wife and daughter. Something that his intuition suggested might not be happening again unless he found this kid

Am I a Monster?

and quick. Sarah did not go all day without speaking to her mother unless she had good reason. Eric turned around and drove back to the station.

"Monica, I need you to do me a favour," he said to his colleague, a magician when it came to tracking addresses and people.

"Anything, Eric. What's up? You look a little stressed."

Eric guessed she was right about that. At thirty-nine, he was already turning grey, his little mop of curly black hair dying on his head prematurely. He'd never been a muscular guy, all bones and no meat his mother liked to say, but he suspected there might be even less soon if Sarah didn't turn up. And his blue eyes were bloodshot most of the time too.

"You could say that. Listen, keep it quiet for now but Tina just phoned me to say Sarah hasn't come home yet and isn't answering her phone. Totally unlike her, so obviously Tina's getting pretty frantic. And to be honest, I'm not feeling good things about this either. Apparently, she met up with a school friend this morning, Andrew something. I assume the same age as Sarah—sixteen. Anyway, can you find out his surname and/or where he lives? They go to Bradwell High School."

"Sure, leave it with me, I'll find him, but you don't think something has happened to your daughter, do you?"

"I hope not, Monica, I really do, but if it has, and this kid has anything to do with it…"

Eric never finished announcing his threat. His throat was constricting already. He left Monica to do her magic and headed off to the canteen to grab a coffee. A strong one. Once he had it in his hands, he sat at a table by himself contemplating all possible scenarios. It was now past eleven, no calls from Tina which meant she had no news. Eric had seen enough during his long spell as policeman and detective to know that what his gut was telling was true—Sarah was in trouble. Even when she'd been to friend's birthdays or had sleepovers, the girl always phoned her mother to let her know how she was. They were like best friends, and Eric was immensely proud of the fact that their daughter confided in them about everything. More to her mother than her father, which was normal, but any doubts, questions, and she went to her mother first for answers. She would know her mother would be out of her mind with worry right now. And if it wasn't for needing this information, he would be beside her, comforting her, going over the protocol measures for such situations. But first, he needed that information.

Thanks to Monica, he didn't have to wait very long. She called to him from the door. Eric practically ran to catch up with her. She led him to her desk and sat down, then pointed to the screen.

"Andrew Foreman, sixteen, lives at 23 Parkhurst Street. Only Andrew by that name his age at Bradwell High so didn't take long to find it."

"Thank you so much, Monica. You deserve a medal."

"I'll take a pay rise."

But Eric was already on his way out before he could reply. Parkhurst Street was just a ten-minute walk from his own road so knew exactly where to go. There was a light on in the living room. He rushed down the overgrown, unkept garden and knocked on the door. After a few seconds with no reply he was about to knock again when he heard grumbling and complaining coming from inside. A woman answered the door, standing there in a skimpy nightie that looked like it hadn't been washed for a while. Her long brown hair was wild like the garden, as though trying to replicate the brambles

Am I a Monster?

strewn about the place. Old makeup on her thin face made her look ten years older than what was probably the desired effect. Her lipstick the brightest of reds. Like the colour of her eyes. Eric had seen eyes like that plenty of times from alcoholics and dope smokers. Evidently, she hadn't been expecting a policeman to knock on her door because she closed the door to a tiny gap and covered her ample, sagging breasts with one hand.

"Whadaya want?" she slurred. "Know what time it is?"

"I'm looking for your son, Andrew. I'd like to speak to him about something urgent."

"In trouble again, is he? Well, he ain't here."

"And where can I find him then?"

"I dunno. He barely comes home. Stays with a friend or somethin'. Good riddance."

"Look, I need to speak with him now. Does he have a phone? You got his number?"

"S'ppose so. Hang on."

She closed the door, cursing her son and soon came back with her phone. She gave him the number and slammed the door in his face, not in the slightest bit concerned it seemed that her son might be in trouble. Eric dialled the number while heading back to his car. It was answered almost immediately.

"Yeah? Who is it?"

"Andrew Foreman?"

"Yeah. Who is it?"

"I'm a police officer, I need to speak to you as soon as possible. Where are you?"

"Fu…oh, err, I'm at a friend's house. What's wrong?"

"I'm outside your mother's house. I need you to come here now, or if you like tell me where you are and I'll come to you."

Eric could hear laughing and joking in the

background, but all male voices, no girls. There was an edge to Andrew's voice but the kid was probably stoned or half drunk. Like his mother. He recalled the girl he'd rescued from her father a month ago after being abused. Was this another case, but this time it had been Sarah the one Andrew had taken his rage out on?

"Err, no, it's okay, I'm just round the corner. Be there in five." He hung up.

Eric's mind was a whirlwind of possibilities, thoughts and possible outcomes. He didn't sound like a kid that had kidnapped or hurt his daughter, not coming so fast like that. He would have expected the kid to make an excuse, that he was out of town or too far way, give himself time to come up with an excuse or alibi. Part of him did want the kid to confess to having hurt Sarah because if he had nothing to do with it, the descent into the unknown was a very real one. And that was even more terrifying. Without Andrew having knowledge of her whereabouts, it meant checking all Sarah's friends, the neighbours, search parties, filing a missing person's report…That would break Tina. At the very least, this kid might know where she was or with who she had been if it wasn't Andrew. He was Eric's one and only hope.

He glanced at his watch. Only two minutes had passed but it seemed like two hours. He spun in circles looking for the kid. The streets were deserted, not a soul outside on this cold night. Deserted like his hopes of a resolution to this nightmare. And then he saw him, walking fast towards him, hands in his pockets, wearing a hoodie. He assumed it was him anyway. The kid stopped when he reached Eric.

"You Andrew Foreman?"

"Yeah. What's wrong?"

The next two or three seconds were imperative. Sarah's life could depend on it.

Am I a Monster?

"My daughter hasn't come home or is answering her phone and she was with you this morning. Sarah Greenwood. Where is she?"

Eric was searching for the tell-tale twitch of an eye, a glance at the floor perhaps as the boy mumbled an answer. To start fiddling with the buttons on his coat, but he got none of that. Instead, Andrew's eyes widened, then he frowned.

"Shit. You're joking, right? I swear, sir, we met for coffee this morning at Daphne's Diner, just ten minutes away, then we went for a walk, and, I dunno, maybe an hour later she left. Said something about having to send an email to the publishers of her book. I haven't seen her since. She said she'd text me tonight or tomorrow. Oh fuck, man. I'm sorry, but I don't know where she is."

Eric stared into the boy's eyes looking for hints of a lie, while at the same time his heart slowly crumbled in his chest and slipped down to his stomach. The boy looked completely genuine and shocked.

"So what time did you split up? And Daphne's Diner, you say?"

"Absolutely. You can ask Daphne herself, she served us coffee. Umm, I guess it would have been around three she left, headed back home, I assume. Shit. You think something bad has happened to her?"

"Her mother last spoke with her this morning when she left to meet you. She hasn't responded to any calls since. Now, if you're not telling me the truth and something has happened to her I will pers—"

"I swear! Look, I'll help you find her. Phone her friends. I'll do it right now."

"Wait. When I phoned, you weren't at home. Your mother says you're barely at home anymore, so where were you when I phoned?"

All the time Eric was studying his face, the way he

dressed, presented himself. After seeing the condition Andrew's mother was in, he had expected a kid to be dressed in hand-me-downs, perhaps filthy and torn, eyes bloodshot and stoned, but he looked just like any normal kid. Short blonde hair, face free from acne or any other blemishes that haunted teens, piercing blue eyes that he assumed the girls would love and dressed in clean jeans and a black jacket. His breath smelt faintly of alcohol, but Eric wasn't so naïve to believe all kids were like Sarah. It was Saturday night, after all, and he knew that kids nowadays started early in almost everything compared to when he'd been that age. If Sarah had brought this boy home and presented him as a friend or boyfriend, Eric would not have complained too much.

"I was at a friend's house. That's where I spend most of my time. My mother drinks too much sometimes so I prefer to keep out of her way."

Eric was also not so naïve to believe everything he heard. It wouldn't be the first kidnapping case to have hit the village.

"Five minutes away, huh?"

"Yeah, just round the corner."

"Can I see it? You know, just to take you off the suspect list."

Andrew seemed to think about it for a few seconds, which made Eric suspicious and also in a way, hopeful. All he wanted for now was to know where his daughter was. In what condition, was something he could think about afterwards.

"Yeah, I guess so. But..."

"But what?"

"Well, you're a police officer and I know we're underage, but everyone drinks beer nowadays at our age and well, maybe the odd joint too, so—"

"Son, right now, I don't give a shit if you're all

Am I a Monster?

mainlining and snorting vodka. I just want to find my daughter."

"Ah, right. Yeah. Okay, then."

Andrew led him back to the flat. When they entered, there were four other boys and a girl, all more or less the same age he figured. An abrupt silence followed as soon as they all caught Eric in his uniform. Smiles and giggles turned to looks of concern and worry.

"It's Sarah's dad. My friend who I saw this morning. Sarah's gone missing. He just wanted to make sure she isn't here."

The kids all looked at each other, some still trying to slyly conceal a joint or can of beer in their hands. The room stank of marijuana. It was as if Eric had walked into a cloud, so thick was the room with smoke. But right now, he couldn't care less.

"Any of you seen her?" asked Eric.

They all shook their heads.

"You're welcome to check the rest of the flat," said Andrew. "It isn't mine, it's Paul's." He pointed to a boy who was evidently Paul. "But anything to help find her, right?"

The kids muttered something resembling an agreement. Eric checked every room, under the beds, inside the wardrobes, but he'd already known what the result would be. What was he going to tell Tina now?

"I'm sorry," said Andrew when Eric returned. "If we see or hear anything we'll be sure to let you know. I'm gonna call all Sarah's friends right now. If they've seen her I'll phone you straight away."

"Okay, thanks. And I'm going to need a list of those names anyway, so I may be phoning you again tomorrow."

Dejected, for the first time in years, Eric felt like crying. Also, for the first time since he could remember, he really did not want to go face his wife right now. But he had no choice. It was the longest drive of his life as he headed to tell Tina the bad news.

Am I a Monster?

Chapter 8

Andrew had known Sarah's father was a cop because she'd told him but even so, he's still been quite surprised it had been him on the other end of the phone the night before. He would need to be careful. It had never occurred to him Sarah might have told her mother or father she was meeting with him Saturday morning. As far as he was aware, no one knew they had agreed to meet. The only possibility that he had thought of was maybe Sarah had phoned or texted her best friend to tell her about being nearly raped. He knew Shelly, knew she had quite a reputation at school for flirting and more with other boys. Andrew had had his eyes on her for a while before overhearing Sarah that day. But no other kids from school had texted him, informing him that his name was currently being thrown around the school like a bad smell, which meant Sarah hadn't told Shelly. The girl had probably gone home and cried herself to sleep. It had only been Andrew's powers of persuasion that had convinced Sarah to meet again so he could explain himself.

But he thought he had been pretty cool and calm when the cop called him. Letting him come to his friend's flat and seeing for himself that Sarah wasn't there had been a spark of genius. And the only reasons that had happened was because they all planned to go back to his own flat and give Sarah a good fucking. A matter of minutes had been the difference. Even so, he was now on the man's radar. As the last person to see her alive, they would be visiting him again at some point, no doubt dragging him down to the station to be interrogated too, so he would have to be careful. Not do anything rash or stupid. He'd have to speak to the guys as well; if he was going to involve them—and they already knew about it—he'd have to make sure they kept their mouths closed. As soon as they'd fucked her, it wouldn't matter; they'd be as guilty as he was.

Because her dad had showed up unexpectedly, Andrew hadn't seen Sarah since yesterday afternoon when he left her tied to the bed. Almost twenty-four hours. He wondered what he would find as he headed there, constantly looking around to make sure he wasn't being followed yet trying to appear inconspicuous at the same time. He had no intentions of letting her go but he also didn't want her dying on him at the same time—he had plans for Sarah and these plans were for a long duration. He thought briefly of buying her something to eat but there had to be some stale bread or something lying about in the flat somewhere—plenty good enough. He might need a mask though; she would probably have shit herself by now.

Andrew gave another quick glance around to make sure no one was watching him and entered the block of flats. His was on the second floor, another three flats on the same floor so a certain discretion was also required. Wouldn't do any good to have the girl screaming all day and night. Fortunately, though, on one side of his flat was the lift, and on the other a room used to store cleaning stuff, so he had no direct neighbours on the other side of the walls.

Tentatively, he opened the front door and stepped in, holding his breath in case a nasty smell awaited him. But it was quiet inside and no odour of shit and piss wafting to suffocate him. Maybe she was already dead and had totally fucked up his plans. He hurried to the bedroom and burst in. She recoiled as he entered the room, still in the same spot as he'd left her, her sock still taped to her

Am I a Monster?

mouth. Her face was red and puffy as were her eyes so she'd evidently been doing a lot of crying and probably trying to push the sock out with her tongue so she could scream. It was stuffy in the room, Andrew having closed the window before he left and there was a sharp tang in the room. When he checked the bed there was a wet patch beneath her. Fortunately, she hadn't shit herself though. Yet.

"Hey, Sarah. How's it going? Listen, I'm sorry I couldn't come earlier but you told your parents you were with me yesterday, so obviously being the last person to see you your dad came looking for me. But don't worry, I managed to get rid of him. We'll have to be careful though, from now on, so I'll need you to be real quiet. Okay?"

He tore off the duct tape and pulled the sock out of her mouth. She began panting heavily, deep breaths. It must have been terrible for her, breathing through her nose for over twenty-four hours. He was surprised she hadn't fallen unconscious through lack of oxygen. Her eyes lit up when he mentioned her parents, but a look of despair appeared on her face when he told he'd avoided arrest.

"Please, let me go, Andrew. No…No one has to know. I understand you were angry for me pushing you over. I get it. I would have been the same, but look, things got out of hand and now you're worried I'll get you in trouble. But I won't, I promise. I just want to go home."

Fucking bitch. Did she not ever learn? Did she really think he was going to fall for that line? The second he untied her she'd be screaming for help. And as soon as her father got his hands on him, Andrew would be wishing he was in prison, after all. But she didn't need to know his thoughts. Let her believe he was thinking about it. Psychological torture. He'd read about that in school and was fascinated by the subject.

"It's okay, Sarah, I forgive you for that. I understand. I was obnoxious and drunk. I probably deserved it."

Her eyes lit up again. He could see the hope in her eyes, almost a physical thing that he might reach out and snatch away again. Her arms were still above her head, tied to the bed which meant the circulation to her wrists must have gone ages ago. They were probably numb, no feeling to them whatsoever and he was tempted to undo the rope, but he had read about people in terrible situations possessing abnormal strength. All it would take was one good kick to the balls and he would be in serious trouble. More than Sarah. Almost.

"I'm not angry, Andrew, or anything. We can laugh about it another day. But please, I'm really hungry and thirsty and my mother will be panicking big time. Just untie me now. I'll go home, have something to eat and a shower then text you."

Andrew pretended to think about it. He made to untie her wrists, making a show of how tough it was to undo the knot. There was a smile on Sarah's face, a desperate one, her eyes lit up gleaming bright, and he could read her thoughts as if she was saying them out loud. He stopped and scratched his chin.

"You know what? I was thinking. I kinda liked fucking you yesterday, and you do look pretty cute there. If it hadn't been for your dad turning up like that, we were all gonna come and fuck you. So, I think I'll leave you where you are. Just seeing you like that, legs spread, it's like you're begging for another. You are, aren't you, you little tease."

"What? Wait, no! Andrew, please, don't do this!"

Andrew pulled his trousers down, proudly showing her the erection already ready for action.

Am I a Monster?

"You bastard! You fucking bastard! My dad will fucking kill you when he catches you. You better let me go now, or—"

Andrew punched her in the mouth, splitting her lips. He then got on top of her and rammed his cock inside of her. Despite her struggling and writhing there was no stopping him. All the time, he stared at her face, smiling and winking. She spat at him, a big blob of reddish saliva that dribbled down his chin. He scooped it up and wiped it over her face. He made sure to ram her as hard as he could when he came, causing her head to crack against the headboard. She was in tears already, having given up with her empty threats.

Panting, he climbed off her and pulled his trousers up. She was crying heavily now, panicking, hysterical, begging for her mother and for her father to come and get her. In that moment she looked five years younger. Except for one thing. It gave him an idea. He took out his phone and called his friend, Dave. Dave and the other members of their little clan were in the other flat. He told him he had a surprise for them and that they should come over. When he hung up, he smiled at Sarah.

"They're on their way. You get to meet my friends. I think you'll find 'em real sweet. Even Karen, Dave's girlfriend. But I think we need to do something before they get here. Make you look real sexy and cute."

He headed off to the bathroom and came back with a set of tweezers he usually used for his nostril hairs. Then, crouching at the foot of the bed, he pulled out her pubic hairs one by one until she was completely bald down there. Sarah screamed with every tug until she'd screamed herself hoarse. Hearing her wheezing, he remembered the girl hadn't had anything to drink since yesterday morning. He went and fetched a glass and half filled it with warm water from the tap. When he returned, he squeezed her cheeks together until her mouth opened then slowly poured the water in. She swallowed it eagerly.

"There, that'll keep you going for a while. I'll give ya something to eat later though. Don't want you getting fat on us, do we?"

There was a loud ringing. Someone had rung the bell. He went to check and let his friends in and led them to the bedroom.

"Woah, what the fuck? You weren't joking!" said Dave.

They all laughed at the helpless girl lying there, looking as though some demon or monster had just walked in. Four of Andrew's friends gawped at Sarah, plus Karen who chuckled. All of them shared secrets together, no one hid nothing from each other. They had all done bad things together, all came from poor families, and all of them were sick of everything. All they wanted out of life was some fun and fuck everyone else.

"Told ya, didn't I! That cute or what? This bitch ain't going nowhere after what she did to me. Especially seeing as her dad's a pig. I just give her a good'un. Who's next?"

It took considerable debate as to what order things would be done in, but an orderly line was formed, each friend cheering the other on as they undressed and fucked Sarah. She closed her eyes each time, grimacing, sobbing, begging it to stop. Occasionally, she would look pleadingly at Karen as if by being another girl she would understand better the suffering and humiliation she was being put through. Andrew watched her closely. Karen laughed most of the time but failed to make eye contact with Sarah. When the last of his friends, Kevin, pulled his trousers down, they all whistled. His dick would have made a few porn actresses wince. He

Am I a Monster?

climbed on top of her, entered her and twisted her nipples as he fucked her, then pulling her breasts as though trying to tear them off. They were red raw by the time he came inside her. And when he did come inside her, he leaned over and bit one of her nipples, drawing blood.

"That's for hurtin' my mate, bitch," said Kevin, then slapped her across the face. Sarah could barely cry anymore, so exhausted was she.

"What about you, Karen? Wanna lick some wet pussy?"

"What? No, thank you! Maybe another day. She fucking stinks!"

If Sarah thought it was over, she was very wrong in her assumptions. Andrew went and grabbed a six pack. They sat around joking and taunting Sarah while drinking beer, occasionally slapping her, pulling at her breasts and nipples. And an hour later when they'd finished another beer, they all took turns to fuck her again. Andrew was proud of his friends.

Chapter 9

Sarah didn't know if it was the humiliation of being gangbanged by strangers or the intense throbbing of her vagina that hurt the most. If pressed, she would probably settle for her vagina, because right now it felt as though someone had thrust their arm up there tearing the delicate lining of the walls. Underneath her was sticky and she was pretty sure it wasn't just their semen seeping from her. She had a pretty good idea it was blood too. She couldn't close her legs even if she wanted. When she had lost her virginity to Carl that had been fun, a little painful at first but later she had been in heaven. This time she was in hell. The area had still been hurting her badly after Andrew pulled all her pubic hairs out. She thought she might faint after the first few had been removed, so to then be subjected to all that, she didn't know such pain could exist.

The humiliation of being gangraped had also been excruciating. She had tried to focus on other things, her mansion and best-selling books but it had been impossible. Then she had tried to telepathically reach out to the girl standing there watching. As another girl, surely she had to feel a little compassion for what was going on but she wouldn't even meet her stare when she tried. She was as bad as her friends. Worse, if anything. She could have told them to stop, just let Sarah go but she had egged them on as much as the other boys. If she ever got out of this, Sarah figured she was going to need a lot of therapy. She'd never want sex again.

Even her breasts and nipples were on fire right now from where that arsehole had twisted them. The guys were sadistic and it had been in that moment Sarah

Am I a Monster?

realised she was in a lot of trouble. They had all left together an hour ago and she still couldn't stop the tears from running down her cheeks, cry out for her mother and father to come and find her. Her throat was on fire also, it seemed like her whole body one way or the other. The water Andrew had poured down her throat did nothing to alleviate the dehydration. And Sarah had an idea that unless she did something, it wasn't going to get any better. In fact, it might get a hell of a lot worse. Fatally, even.

Her father had instilled in her from a very early age to be strong, don't let bullies beat her down, stand up for herself, never give in. Well, right now, not only did it seem she didn't have much choice in the matter, but after being stuck here for over twenty-four hours and violently raped, she was beginning to think her father's advice had not been geared towards situations like this. The way things were going it seemed a very likely possibility she was going to die here.

No, you're not, Sarah. She could hear her father's stern words in her head. *You're not just going to lie here and give up. Wait to die. I taught you better than that. Remember what happened before. If you at least try it's better than giving up. C'mon, check those knots again. He's a kid. How would he know how to tie proper knots? They've had their sick fun, they won't be back for a while. Give it a shot.*

She tugged on the ropes around her wrists, but knew she was wasting her time already. What was the point? One didn't need to be a sailor to know how to tie a knot. She'd already lost most blood flow to her wrists so they were now numb, pins and needles the only sign they were still attached to her body. She gave another weak tug and gave up. She was going to die as an unpublished author. Her dream of making a career out of this was over before it had even started.

You'll die if you just lay there doing nothing, girl. You wanna live or not? I've seen kids younger than you survive much worse, so stop feeling sorry for yourself and try harder!

Sarah bit back the tears and tried to push herself up so she could at least get some blood flowing to her wrists. It was tough and she thought her spine might snap in the process but after a little contorting of her body, she was almost sitting upright. Her arms were bent back behind her, but she could feel the blood rushing to her wrists again. It was like an adrenaline rush. She managed to twist her neck so she could see the knots holding her to the bed. As her father had suggested, simple, crude knots, same as she used to tie her shoelaces but without the fancy bows. An idea occurred to her. Sarah leaned over, straining the groaning muscles in her neck, the veins throbbing, and gripped one of the knots between her teeth.

Slowly, Sarah. I know you're starting to panic but take your time. Don't go pulling a muscle. Slowly and carefully wins the day.

She hadn't quite realised but now that it was said, yes, she could feel the panic in her body, sending bolts of both excitement and desperation through her veins. She wanted to just gnaw through the fucking rope, and spit it out, twist her body that little bit more, but if she did, muscles would be pulled, and it would all be over. Resisting the urge to let panic take control was the hardest thing she had ever done in her life. But somehow, she managed to do so. Slowly and gently, she tugged at one of the lengths of thin rope, pulling it centimetre by centimetre, until finally it came loose. By wiggling her wrist, the rope fell to the floor. She was free. Ten seconds later she was completely free.

Am I a Monster?

Quickly, telling herself to keep calm, not to panic, she put on her jeans, top and trainers that were still over in the corner. Twice she had to grab onto the wall to stop herself from falling over; her legs weak and buckling beneath her, her head dizzy from lack of food and water. She took deep breaths, willed her heart to slow down. Andrew had taken her phone and smashed it so that was no good, so instead, she made her way to the front door. If necessary, once she was outside she would scream with everything she had should Andrew appear or one of his friends. She wasn't even going to risk knocking on a neighbour's door, ask them for help, in case they were friends of his. For all she knew one of those that had raped her lived in the same block. Sarah opened the front door and stepped outside, tears streaming for her fortune and for her father's wise words.

"What the fuck?"

Andrew stood there, holding a shopping bag. For a few seconds both stared at each other, in shock. It was Andrew who reacted first, pushing Sarah roughly so she tripped over her feet and fell. Her reaction was immediate. Screaming for help as loud as she could, she pushed herself up, ready to fight to the death if required. There was no way she was being tied up on that bed again. She brought a leg back to kick him in the balls, but Andrew was just a little too quick for her. Before her foot could connect, his fist did so with her nose, breaking it once again. Sarah's legs buckled for good this time and she crashed to the floor.

She woke up an undetermined amount of time later. As she slowly regained her senses, she tried to sit up but found it impossible to do so. When she swivelled her head, she was horrified to find herself once again naked and tied to the bed.

"Well, I gotta say, bonus points for effort, Sarah. I

don't know how you managed to get free, but good job I came back in time, right? We can't have you go running around screaming for help, so I figured we better do somethin' about it."

He bent down and picked something up off the floor. Sarah strained to see what, her heart thudding in her chest, terrified for what was about to happen. Andrew stood over her at the bottom of the bed with a hammer in his hands.

"Wait, no, I'm sorry. Please don't. I'm sorry. It won't happen again. I—" She howled as he brought the hammer down on her toe. She howled a lot more as he subsequently smashed it into the rest of them. Bolts of agony shot up her legs. Her bladder and bowels gave way. She shook on the bed as if suffering an epileptic fit. But still he wasn't finished.

"Now, here's the deal, Sarah. I really didn't want to have to do this, but you've left me with no choice. You've been a naughty girl and naughty girls have to be punished. They have to learn right from wrong and sometimes, as my dad used to teach me, the hard way is the only way. So, if you ever want to get out of here and be that hotshot author you've always dreamed of, this is the deal; if you ever try to break free again, I will do to your hands what I'm about to do to your feet. One at a time. You'll never write again."

He dropped the hammer and picked up a pair of pliers. Sarah was barely conscious, her feet on fire, every time she involuntarily shuddered it was as if someone had poured molten lead onto her toes. In one hand, Andrew gripped the big toe of her right foot. With the other he squeezed and twisted it with the pliers until there was a snapping sound. He let go then gripped the next toe. When he reached her little toe and twisted with the pliers, he almost tore the thing off. Blood spurted from

Am I a Monster?

where the bone had snapped, her toe bent backwards, facing her, bone jutting out. He then did the same thing to her other foot.

Her vision was fading fast. She was swimming in and out of consciousness, wishing she could just die right now and forget everything her father had told her. But before she did finally fall unconscious Andrew pulled down his trousers and raped her once more. She was out cold before he finished.

Chapter 10

Eric had consoled his wife for as long as he was able after returning home from speaking with Andrew and checking his flat. As long as possible because all he wanted to do was get back out on the streets to look for his daughter. But he couldn't leave his wife alone in the house, suffering immensely. He thought of friends or relatives she could stay with or that might come and keep her company, but she had insisted that no, she wasn't going anywhere in case Sarah came staggering through the door and didn't want anyone's company either. Instead, she took a Valium to help with her nerves and after a while she had fallen asleep through sheer exhaustion. Eric covered her with a blanket on the sofa and headed back out, patrolling the streets, stopping bus and taxi drivers to ask them if they'd seen anything suspicious, or a young girl wandering the streets, in shock or dazed. All available units from the station were also out checking all the nightclubs, areas where kids liked to hang out, questioning everyone, but it was as if she had disappeared. And now, Monday morning, their levels of desperation had reached new heights; if Sarah had gotten herself injured somewhere or had been involved in an accident, she would have been found by now. No one of her name or description was in hospital, none of Sarah's friends had any idea where she was. It could only mean one thing, something Eric refused to accept.

But almost forty-eight hours had passed since Sarah was last seen and Eric also knew perfectly well the first forty-hours were crucial. He'd barely slept in that time, snatching the odd hour here and there and Tina was near

Am I a Monster?

breaking point. She looked to have aged ten years over night, her long black hair reminiscent of an old witch from some horror movie, straggled and wild. Everyone, of course, knew now that Sarah was missing and neighbours and family members made a point of staying close to Tina while Eric was out searching. Now it was time to initiate the second stage.

Detectives were now on the case. Eric arrived at the station early and was immediately called to DI Ronald West's office, who would be in charge of the investigation. He was a well-built man, over six feet tall, cropped, black hair that was greying at the sides. He bore a thick moustache too which privately Eric had always thought a little ridiculous, making him look like some shady Mexican or seventies' porn star, but he would never dare say anything to his face. Ronald's eyes were small and beady, darting everywhere, seeing everything, missing nothing. Eyes that had seen many horrors in the man's thirty-plus years on the force. His track record was second to none. Word had it that even those imprisoned at Northgate Hospital for the Criminally Insane feared him. He was both cunning and ruthless and couldn't care less if his suspect was a violent psychopath or a little teen girl—Ronald didn't take shit from no one.

"Eric, I'm sorry to hear about this, we'll do everything we can to find her. I need you to sit down and tell me everything. From the last time you saw her, names of all friends and acquaintances, anyone who might know where she has been."

Eric responded, telling him about Andrew, visiting the flat, and everywhere he'd been looking for her. Ronald seemed especially interested in Andrew, being the last person to have seen her.

"I'm telling you. If I thought there was the slightest hint of anything suspicious about the kid, I would have dragged him here there and then. But he looked genuinely shocked himself. It was him that phoned me later that night and gave me the number to all Sarah's friends. I got each and every one of them out of bed and asked if they'd seen her. All said no. Her best friend, Shelly, knew about Sarah and Andrew seeing each other and it was hardly a secret. I checked Daphne's Diner, spoke to the woman herself and she said they were acting exactly as expected from two teens, laughing and joking."

"So, your daughter and this Andrew meet at Daphne's for lunch. He says around three they both went their separate ways. No one has seen her since. That on its own makes me suspicious. Not a single person who knows your daughter remembers seeing her head home? It takes, what, twenty minutes or so? Someone, somewhere, had to have seen her. Perhaps talking to someone. I hate to say it, Eric, but maybe someone saw her talking to some stranger in a car? In this day and age everyone carrying mobile phones and recording everything, nothing goes unnoticed. I want to speak to this Andrew kid myself, but I think it's time to set up a press conference, get the media involved."

A shiver rippled through Eric's tired body. He knew it had been coming and he knew it was the next best thing if he was to find his daughter alive, but it was also like a confirmation. That this wasn't some bad dream or his daughter had simply lost track of time, was innocently sitting in some friend's house talking about boys and futures. It was real. It meant him and probably Tina, because she would want to have her say as well, sitting in front of a crowd of strangers telling them their worst nightmare while asked generic questions and their faces photographed dozens of times. The journalists wouldn't understand the terror they were currently living in; all

Am I a Monster?

they would be thinking was the headline for next day's front page. Who they could start interrogating themselves to get the juiciest story from. And all the time Tina would probably be sitting there sobbing while Eric looked on solemnly and begged for information. He'd seen it on TV a thousand times, trying to imagine how they must be feeling. Well, now he knew.

He sighed. "You're right. I've exhausted every possibility. Someone saw something, so yeah, get it done. You want me to bring Andrew in for further questioning?"

"Yes. He's our only lead right now, so maybe there's something he forgot. I want to know what they spoke about before separating. Your daughter was going to have a book published, right?"

"Yes, she got the email just the day before she went missing. I've never been so proud. Why?"

"Because it means there's no way in hell she would have ran off or anything stupid if the press asks. Not that I expect that from her anyway, but questions will be asked. I'll set the press conference up for this afternoon. In the meantime, bring me this Andrew kid."

Eric agreed and headed off to find him. He should be in school, where no doubt the news would now be known by all, teachers and kids alike. When he reached Bradwell High and spoke to the receptionist he could feel all eyes on him, the whispering behind his back, nudging of kids to each other as they walked past. He had half a mind to turn around and scream at them, to stop looking at him as though some kind of freak, but somehow he managed to keep his calm until the headmaster arrived. He told the man of his intentions, listened to his condolences as though Sarah was already dead, and waited for Andrew.

He didn't look at all surprised when he was brought

to Eric. In fact, he rushed over to him.

"Any news yet, sir? I haven't heard anything on the news or anything, so was hoping she'd been found. She has been found, right?"

There certainly appeared to be a note of expectancy on his face, a touch of desperation for good news, but when Eric's own features failed to materialise into a glowing, relieved smile, Andrew's faded rapidly.

"Wait, you mean…you mean she's still *missing*?"

"Yes, she is. It's partly why I'm here. There'll be a press conference this afternoon and the matter has been handed over to the Serious Crime Squad. As the last person to see her they want to speak with you. Now. I'm here to pick you up and take you to the station. Now, as a minor, you can refuse unless accompanied by an adult if you wish, your mother or some other, but they just want to ask you some questions about Saturday afternoon, that's all."

"Oh no, that's fine. My mother's probably still asleep anyway and she'd get annoyed if I woke her and made her come. I'll be happy to help anyway I can, sir."

"Good. Let's go, then."

Eric so badly wanted Andrew to be guilty of having kidnapped her. To have her tied up somewhere, unhurt, waiting to be rescued. If Andrew turned to him right now and confessed he wouldn't even be angry with the boy, just relieved. The anger would come later, of course.

They arrived at the station and Eric led the kid to Ronald's office. He knocked on the door and stepped in when told. Ronald's office was sparse but neat, a few awards and decorations on the walls, photos of his wife and kids on his desk. A pile of files and papers sat neatly stacked to one side. Eric had no idea if they were cases he was currently working on or something completely different. He didn't ask either.

Am I a Monster?

"Sir, this is Andrew Foreman. Sarah's friend, the last one to see her Saturday afternoon."

"Sit down, Andrew."

No hello, apologies from taking him out of school, straight to business. Ronald scrutinised the kid top to bottom, no expression on his face, nothing. Eric liked that. If anyone was going to make the kid trip up, it was Ronald.

"Obviously, you know why you're here. I want you to tell me everything leading up to the last time you saw Sarah. You met her the night before as well, I understand. Tell me where you went, what you discussed, leave nothing out."

Andrew recounted everything exactly as he'd told Eric, who was standing behind the boy checking his notes as Andrew explained their actions.

"Then, at around three I guess, she said she had to write an email to the people publishing her book. We said we'd text each other then meet up at school on Monday. I haven't seen her since."

Ronald never took his eyes off Andrew during the ten minutes or so he gave his story. Eric didn't think the man had even blinked. But Andrew's story concurred exactly as he'd told Eric.

"Did you do anything to her, Andrew?"

It was so sudden it even surprised Eric.

"What? Me? No, I didn't. I'm just as shocked she's missing as everyone else. I really liked her. I was so excited for her to become a published author. If you set up a search party or anything, I'd like to offer my help. My friends will help too."

"You barely live with your mother. Why?"

Andrew sighed. "My dad left when I was younger. He used to drink and get aggressive with the both of us. Since he left, my mother kinda got depressed. Started drinking too. Now, she's almost as bad as he was, so I prefer to spend time at a friend's flat. Soon as school finishes this summer, I'm gonna look for a job and move out for good. Can't wait."

There was nothing else to say. Ronald sat staring at Andrew for a while, saying nothing, no doubt trying to unnerve him. It didn't work. Eventually, Ronald told him about the press conference and that he could be present if he wished, say a few words even. Andrew fervently agreed that he would.

Eric offered to drive him back to school but the kid said no, he'd walk. It was almost lunch time anyway. He left leaving Eric and Ronald alone.

"What did you think? Sounds legit to me. His story is exactly as he told me, even to the times they met and left. Didn't seem nervous at all as you'd expect from a kid."

"People, even kids, can be deceiving, good actors, but in this case, I'm inclined to agree. I'll have someone watching him though, just in case. Sorry, Eric, but all we can do now is set up that press conference and hope we get a tip."

Eric agreed, but his hope had long since left him. He wondered how long Tina would be able to cope with losing her little girl if no one came forward.

As expected, the small room used for press conferences was packed. Full of jostling journalists crammed shoulder to shoulder. It was as if they were in a nightclub—so many camera flashes it might have been a strobe light constantly going off. Anyone susceptible to epilepsy might have been in serious trouble. But fortunately, that was one of the very few things Eric and Tina did not have to worry about. They sat at a table, Ronald next to them and an enlarged photo of Sarah behind them. Tina had practically shuffled to the station from the car, helped along by Eric as though she was

Am I a Monster?

elderly and crippled. Her eyes were terribly puffed and red. Family members of both were also present at the conference—having refused to leave Tina's side since they received the news. It had been months since he'd seen both his brother, aunt and uncle, and Tina's family members. It was always depressing, he thought, the way families only got together in moments of extreme happiness or sadness. Having all those people around made him feel claustrophobic in his own home. Most of them hadn't even bothered coming for Christmas.

"You ready for this, Tina?"

She nodded. "No, but I just want my baby back. What if nothing comes of this? What if they get no calls, no tips? Then what are we going to do?"

"Keep your hopes up, Tina. Someone will have seen or heard something, I'm sure of it."

"What about that boy? I know he had something to do with it. You should have seen Sarah's face when she came home early Friday night. You have questioned him again, haven't you?"

"Twice, Tina. And his story checks out."

"Then where is she?" she practically screamed. All eyes turned to her briefly, then looked away, perhaps out of respect. Tina barely seemed aware she'd yelled. She sobbed on Eric's shoulder.

Andrew was also sitting across from them, looking distraught, fidgeting on his chair, picking at his fingernails. In a way, Eric felt sorry for him too. He seemed a nice kid and if it was true he had nothing to do with Sarah's disappearance, he had every right to be here also. They may not have been boyfriend and girlfriend but that didn't make it hurt any less.

"Ladies and gentlemen, we require your help. A girl, sixteen-year-old Sarah Greenwood, went missing Saturday afternoon and there has been no contact with her since. Naturally, both ourselves and her parents are extremely worried about what may have happened to her and we request any and all help in trying to locate her," said Ronald.

Tina continued sobbing. Her handkerchief was already soaking wet with tears. As if she'd soaked it in the sink first before bringing it with her. More camera flashes, journalists holding mobile phones like microphones, others furiously jotting down stuff. Many already had hands in the air ready to ask the usual questions. Eric knew the importance of this but just wanted to get out. It made him sick the indifference shown by the reporters. All they cared about was a heart wrenching photo for the front page which they probably already had in Eric and his wife's faces.

As expected, questions were directed at them all. Ronald answered them individually, given detailed descriptions of the clothes she was wearing, the fact she was about to be a published author, so no way would she have run off. Then, the dreaded moment when Eric and his wife were invited to speak directly to the press. Eric looked at Tina who shook her head. He stood up and headed to the microphone behind him.

"Hi. Umm, thank you all for coming. As you now know, our beloved daughter has been missing for over seventy-two hours. I'm a policeman so I know what that means. Please, I urge anyone who may have information on her whereabouts or thinks they may have seen her with somebody Saturday afternoon, please come forward. The slightest bit of information could help us find her.

"She had just received confirmation the day before that a novel she wrote was going to be published, so she was extremely excited. It was all she could think about, so there's not a chance she left without telling anyone.

Am I a Monster?

Please, if you saw her talking to someone, get in a vehicle, anything, please phone the hotline, anonymously if you wish. We just want our daughter back safe and sound. Thank you."

Eric sat back down and gripped his wife's trembling hand. "You want to say something too?"

"I can't. Not yet."

Eric turned to Ronald and shook his head, then looked to Andrew and nodded. Andrew approached the microphone. "I…I, umm, would just like to say the same as Mr Greenwood. We were…are friends at school. We went out for a pizza Friday night and had a great time. So much so, we met up again Saturday at midday. We had another chat then she left around three to go home. That was the last time anyone saw her. I…I was the last person to see her. I can't sleep at nights knowing that, that maybe I could have done something, like maybe it was my fault in some way. Like, I should have accompanied her home. If it wasn't for me, she might still be here. So…so please, someone saw something. I know it. Please come forward. I just want to see her again."

Andrew burst out crying, covering his face with both hands as the reporters frantically snapped off photos, each flash of their powerful cameras making Eric jump. Poor kid, he thought. He hadn't considered Andrew might blame himself for her disappearance. Might be an idea to invite him over for dinner now and again, he told himself. With no parents to console him, the kid was at the mercy of his private thoughts, no one to confide in except stoned, half-drunk friends. Life just wasn't fair. He prayed he caught the son of a bitch who took her. If anything happened to his little girl, he'd cut the fucker's balls off when he caught him.

Chapter 11

Now that her feet were virtually crushed and useless, Andrew had untied her from the bed and left her there confident she wasn't going anywhere. The slightest attempt at escape or screaming for help, he had made it quite clear the consequences. And of course, it wasn't just Andrew anymore. It was also his friends. Sarah might escape and get Andrew arrested, but she didn't know the names or addresses of the others. But Andrew knew where she lived.

He had come to the flat last night and told her about the press conference. Her parents begging for information and he had laughed and seemed especially proud of himself when he told her he too had pretended to be distraught and heartbroken. This nearly broke Sarah's own heart. It hurt as much as her toes did.

"Should have seen it, Sarah. Your dad consoling me, patting me on the back! I had to hold back a chuckle. If only he knew, right? They think you're dead by the way, you know that? So they're gonna be looking in dump sites, fields, abandoned places, and so on. Safer for us, right?"

Sarah broke down after hearing that. She had been trying hard not to let him see how much he was affecting her. She wanted to be strong, not give him the satisfaction of seeing her tears, but Sarah had never been particularly strong anyway. Shelly had always been the strong one, protecting her from the bullies. It seemed strange to think now that she was going to be a published author she had always been lost for words when it came to witty comebacks, but instead, when taunted or bullied as a youngster, she had gotten tongue-tied, her mind

Am I a Monster?

blank. Shelly could throw out the creative insults and threats at the snap of a finger. She would shrink into herself, too scared of any retaliation if she chose to attack the attacker, but this, hearing that Andrew had publicly laughed at her and her parents in front of the whole world was too much. She covered her face and sobbed until she had nothing left to give.

Andrew found it funny and cute.

After hearing that, his friends had all come over and winced and joked about the state of her toes which were now a yellow-purple colour, broken almost beyond repair. They were swollen too, double the size. They called her a cripple, a freak, prodding at her toes with their fingers or simply kicking her. One stubbed out his cigarette on her little toe and she howled in pain, large blisters forming there. Then they'd taken turns to fuck her. Lightning bolts of agony shot up her every time one of the boys climbed on top of her not caring about her feet as they held her legs in the air. In that moment, she wished she was dead. She could barely breathe thanks to a broken nose. Her vagina throbbed just as badly. She was quite sure a certain amount of damage had been done thanks to the violence with which they had raped her. There had been a leakage afterwards as she lay there strewn on the bed, a trickle of blood seeping onto the cum-stained sheet. The girl, Karen, had cheered them on.

She was here with Sarah now, alone. Both she and her boyfriend, Dave, had popped over after lunch to bring Andrew his dope fix and then Dave and Andrew had left together to go buy something to eat. Sarah was starving herself. Since she'd been kidnapped Andrew had given her just two stale sandwiches, and she was limited to two glasses of warm water a day. Andrew said she had to earn more food if she wanted although what that entailed she didn't know. But now was an opportunity. Just the two girls alone, surely, she could appeal to her better nature. She had to have one.

Karen was sat across the bedroom from Sarah scrolling through her phone. She said she preferred to sit by the window because Sarah stank of piss and cum and sweat. Although she was obviously a girl, from a distance Karen might have been mistaken for a boy. Short, cropped black hair, barely any breasts which if she had were hidden beneath a baggy jumper. She wore no makeup and thick, black glasses made her dark eyes appear even bigger. Her lips were thin, pink strips and a slightly crooked nose made it seem perpetually broken. She always wore trousers too and big boots. Quite what Dave saw in her Sarah didn't know. She was big too as though she spent a lot of time weightlifting in the gym. Her biceps would put many a boy to shame. Sarah began to sob quietly, but this time acting.

"I want to die. I can't go through this anymore. I just want someone to put me out of my misery. I don't care about being an author anymore and I've accepted I'll never see my parents again or have kids, a future. I just want to die. I want someone to kill me now. Karen, will...will you do it for me? Please?"

Karen looked up from her phone. No hint of remorse on her face, Sarah might have been discussing the weather. "What? You want me to kill you? So I go to prison? Sorry, not gonna happen. I ain't no killer."

"But look at me. My feet have been crushed, I'm starving to death and probably pregnant. By who, I don't know. All of them perhaps. If I have a baby, it will either be deformed in some way or they'll kill it too. My body hurts too much—you'll be doing me a favour. You can say I attacked you and you had no choice. They'll dump my body somewhere and I won't care then anyway. But please, you have to help me. They're going to kill me

Am I a Monster?

anyway, so you might as well do it now. Please, Karen."

There was a flicker in Karen's eyes, a twitching of her mouth. Somewhere in there had to be a guilty conscience, a desire to help out a fellow girl. As a girl she must surely be able to appreciate how terrible it would feel to be multiply gangraped. Brutally.

"I can't, Sarah. Look, I'm sorry this is happening, but there's nothing I can do. Just…just hope that Andrew gets bored and lets you go."

"But he won't! He can't now anyway, not after going on TV asking for help in finding me. The whole country will be against him for deceiving them like that. It's happened before. He's never going to let me go and I'm scared what else he'll do to me before he kills me. I'm pretty sure they've ruptured something inside me. I…I don't stop leaking blood, from, like, between my legs. Imagine your worst ever period, but a thousand times more painful. You gotta kill me, Karen, I'm begging you."

Another twitch in Karen's face suggested Sarah's words were getting to her. Karen looked at the crimson stain on the bed and winced. She instinctively brought her legs together.

"I can't, Sarah! I'm not a killer. Look, I don't agree with what they're doing to you, but I can't stop them! They'll do it to me as well and there's no way that's happening. They're all scared of Andrew, even Dave. The kid's a fucking psycho. Always has been. It's all a façade he puts on at school to appear the cool guy but he's not. He used to torture and kill fucking animals when he was a child. That's why his father left—his own father was scared of him. And, of course, no one dares say anything to him, or he'll do the same to them.

"I'm really sorry, Sarah, I am. I wish there was something I could do to help, but when I finish school in the summer, I'm going to university and getting the fuck away from all of them. Just…just hang in there and don't try to piss him off."

"But there is something you can do! You don't want to kill me, fine. I didn't really mean it anyway, but just let me go. I'll crawl outta here. I'll say I hit you over the head when you weren't looking and knocked you out. He won't know. And it was his fault for untying me from the bed.

"If I manage to escape and get help, my dad's a cop, Andrew will go to prison for at least twenty years—he'll see to it. And if I don't get away, I'll say I hit you. Andrew won't blame you; he'll blame himself. Please, I don't want to die without seeing my dreams come true. Without seeing my parents ever again. Just look away and I'll drag myself out. You'll never see me again."

Karen's face contorted into a myriad of features. Sarah could practically hear the possibilities churning in the girl's head. The possible consequences, chances of success, wanting to help a fellow, innocent human being but not wanting to end up like Sarah. She was biting her bottom lip, her phone forgotten and dangling from her hand. It was now or never.

"Please, Karen. The second I'm outside, someone will see me and call an ambulance. From there, the police and Andrew can rot in prison then hell forever."

Sarah dragged herself to the edge of the bed, her feet screaming at her to stop. She ignored it and somehow managed to twist herself around so she could slowly and gently drop to the floor while keeping her legs in the air. Her back would cushion the blow. Karen wasn't even watching her—lost in thought.

"Fuck, okay, but be quick. I'm warning you though, if Andrew catches you before you get the police or an ambulance, I'm telling him you attacked me. I'll hit

Am I a Monster?

myself over the head with something to make it bleed. You're on your own. Good luck."

"Thank you so much, Karen."

Sarah dragged herself across the bedroom floor. Every part of her throbbed in agony but she bit her lip and kept going—her life depended on it. And yet, just as she reached the door and was trying to push herself up to open it, for the second time so close to freedom, she was too late. Laughter came from the other side of the door. It opened and Andrew and his friends walked in.

"Sarah, what are you doing down there?" asked Andrew, perplexed.

She looked up at him, horrified, then at Karen who was pallid.

"I...I was..."

"She said she was fed up with lying on the bed. Wanted to do a little exercise. I told her she was stupid and she was gonna fuck up her feet even more but she wouldn't listen," said Karen quickly.

"Oh dear, Sarah, you are stubborn. We can't have you wandering around the flat, you know. You'll hurt yourself." He picked her up and carried her back to the bed.

Sarah didn't resist, but she also didn't like the way he glared at Karen. Had he guessed her true intentions?

The others piled into the bedroom too, Dave kissing Karen.

"So, been looking to do some exercise, huh? Well, I got just the thing for you. That's exactly what we we're thinking too. Gotta stay healthy, right?"

Sarah's stomach lurched. She didn't like where this was heading at all, or the way he was still glancing at Karen as he spoke. He knew perfectly well Karen had lied to him and for now, Sarah was going to be the one that paid. She prayed he did nothing to Karen—she might have an ally here later, maybe she'd go to the police herself.

"Now, I told you what would happen if you ever tried to escape or anything. I'd crush every bone in your hands then cut them off. And I will. But also, unless you do exactly as I tell you, or anyone here for that matter, I will also make you pay. Bad. You got it?"

She nodded, so scared she was incapable of articulating any word.

"Good."

The others were chuckling and smirking, all with cans of beer in their hands, or lighting up joints.

"So, this is Rob," he said, slapping him on the back. "It's his birthday, so we thought you could give him a little treat. Not a private one though 'cause that wouldn't be fair but I guess he should get to go first afterwards. You up to giving him a little treat, Sarah?"

His previous words echoed in her head. She knew without a doubt, especially after what Karen had told him, that if she refused him or angered him in any way, he would carry out his threat. But what was expected of her now? A blowjob probably. Considering they'd all raped her several times, it was hardly a life-threatening, life-changing request. She could just close her eyes and dream of that mansion she was going to live in one day. She could even write a book about her experiences here—that would surely be a best-seller. True crime was big.

She nodded and waited for Rob to approach and pull his trousers down. But instead, Andrew started fumbling around in a plastic shopping bag he was carrying, the others smirking. Sarah gasped when he threw the object at her.

The dildo had to be thicker than her wrist. The walls of her vagina throbbed in agony at the mere thought of

Am I a Monster?

what was asked of her. When Andrew had allowed her to use the toilet earlier, her urine had been a pinkish colour. If she put that thing inside her, it would surely rupture something.

"What's wrong?" asked Andrew after Sarah had been staring at it for a while.

"I...I can't. It hurts down there already."

Andrew's grin twitched. A flicker in his eyes suggested he was not impressed by her excuse. He looked at Karen. "Whadaya say, Karen? You reckon she could fit it inside her easy enough? Not gonna let Rob down is she?"

Karen laughed. "She's probably had bigger up her arse. I say do it."

Saah was shocked. Ten minutes ago, she had tried to help Sarah escape, and now she was encouraging them again.

"See, Sarah, Karen says you've had bigger up your arse. I bet she's right too. So fucking do it. We ain't got all day."

His eyes were fiery, blazing. If she still refused he probably would kick it up her. She picked it up and spread her legs. The others cheered.

"I want you to fuck yourself with it and pretend it's Rob's dick you got in you. Tell him how much you love it and you want more and harder. If I don't think you're trying hard enough, I'll shove it up your arse myself. Without lubrication."

Her hands trembling, Sarah gripped the toy in both hands but made sure to spit on it first, even though she had virtually no saliva in her mouth. It had been hours since Andrew gave her a glass of water. Even longer since he'd fed her. Somehow, she managed to lubricate it enough so it didn't hurt so bad as she pushed the tip in but the further in it went the more her walls contracted, trying to expel it. She grimaced and winced as she pushed it in more. It must have been about nine inches long and Andrew had told her to push as much as possible in. Her body shuddered. She guessed this was how it must be to have a baby, but without anaesthetic. Sharp stabs reverberated inside her. Then she started pushing it in and out, hissing out Rob's name and saying what she'd been told to say. The boys cheered and clapped, slapping Rob on the back and making lewd comments. Even Karen joined in.

"That feel good, Sarah, huh? You like that?"

"Yes," she croaked. "It feels so good. You're so big, Rob, I'm such a slut."

They were almost in tears now, laughing so hard. Sarah was in tears too, through both pain and shame. Instead of looking at them, she focused on the bed, imagining doing to Andrew what he had threatened to do to her. Right now, the only things on her mind were either dying or swearing that if she got out of this one day, they would all pay for this humiliation. She thought she could feel the walls of her vagina tearing. Every time she pulled the dildo out there was more crimson smeared on it. They told her to continue for another five minutes before Andrew told her she could stop.

"Well done, Sarah. Proud of ya. Now give Rob the blowjob he's been wanting since we got here."

She did as she was told.

Once they'd had their fun, they all left Sarah alone, naked, starving and sobbing. About an hour later, Andrew came back with a sandwich he might have pulled from the rubbish. It had mould on it. He also gave her a lukewarm glass of water and tied one wrist to the bed, using a padlock so she couldn't undo it.

"I know what you were trying to do earlier, Sarah. You can't fool me. I'll speak with Karen in private, but

Am I a Monster?

you try that little stunt again, I'll cut your wrists off. We're off out, have a nice day."

And with that he left. Sarah greedily swallowed each piece of the sandwich as though it was the best thing ever. She cried herself to sleep shortly after.

Chapter 12

Andrew sat by himself at the bar, nursing his second beer. The owner knew he was under eighteen but let him drink anyway, despite the risk to his business. Andrew guessed he did it out of pity—everyone knew about Andrew's mother and the way she had always treated him. No one blamed him for drinking alcohol so early in life. But tonight, Andrew wasn't in his usual good spirits as he normally was in here. Most of the time he behaved himself, not stupid enough to get drunk and cause a scene, getting himself barred in the process. He'd play pool with the locals, always a joke to tell or funny story, usually involving his mother's drunken antics. Even though his upbringing had been shit and he hated his mother, he could normally find some way of using the situation to his benefit. Telling a funny story about his mother falling over shitfaced often earned him another free beer and he wasn't saying no to that.

Tonight, he wasn't in the mood though and the others in the bar seemed to sense it, keeping away from him, leaving him alone. They all knew about Sarah, of course, and had seen him on TV begging for information, sobbing as he did so, and everyone had offered to help in any way they could. Search parties had been discussed. Many knew Sarah's dad also and respected him immensely as an honest cop and it had worn Andrew out having to pretend to be traumatised and grief-stricken all the time. They assumed his quiet moods were because of this. And in a way it was, just not how they thought; Andrew was in a bad mood because he seriously suspected Karen of trying to help Sarah escape.

There was no way Sarah had been trying to do a little

Am I a Monster?

exercise. The girl had to be in great pain after having her toes crushed so what the fuck was she doing dragging herself around the flat then? She also had to be pretty weak after going so long with barely anything to eat. Andrew had noticed the weight loss already, the way her skin was being stretched, her stomach slowly sinking into herself. But what he couldn't understand was why his best friend's girlfriend would betray him and everyone like that. Maybe it was a female thing; seeing another girl treated that way and she felt compassion for her. Girls always were too soft. Except his mother, of course. He really didn't want to do or say anything to Karen and risk everything, but he was going to have to do something. The whole relationship between him and his friends was built on mutual trust. If Sarah ever did get free—and he'd kill her before that happened—they would all go to prison, Karen included. That wasn't going to happen either.

The sad part was that Karen knew he had something of a volatile history so she should have been too scared to help. He could only assume Sarah had gotten to her in ways only another girl could, using her emotions to psychologically blackmail her into helping. That bitch had not only tricked him but had tricked Karen too. Sarah, it seemed, needed to be taught another lesson. A harsh one.

On the TV behind the bar, Sarah's face appeared. He didn't know what the reporter was saying because the volume was turned down, but the task force's hotline number was below Sarah's face and the reporter had a dejected, worried look to her. He imagined the police were asking the local TV stations to not let the locals forget there was a missing girl out there. Her father would be constantly harassing them to help at all times. Well, fuck them. Sarah wasn't going anywhere, but he was. But first, he pulled out his phone and dialled each and every one of his friends, asking them where they were, what they were doing. He did this several times a day when they weren't together, just to ensure he was in control of matters and knew their every move. And also, so that they were fully aware too. He finished his beer and headed back to his flat.

There was a nasty smell in the flat that assaulted him the second he opened the door. That was worrying too. All it needed was some nosy fucking neighbour to knock on the door and it might cause problems. Exactly as what happened to Jeffrey Dahmer in that Netflix documentary he watched a couple of weeks ago. Fucking epic documentary too. Dahmer was his hero. Andrew had always wondered what human flesh tasted like—maybe this was a perfect opportunity to find out. Not with Sarah smelling like that though.

He found her sprawled on the bed staring up at the ceiling, her eyes puffy and bloodshot. Puffy like her toes which were now turning a nasty green colour. Her crooked nose was twisted, dried blood smeared on her cheeks. The bedsheet was filthy too, covered in stains of various sorts. For his own benefit, he was going to have to change them, but that wouldn't make any difference with Sarah's legs covered in dried urine and shit from when he'd broken her toes. She must have diarrhoea or an infection of some kind because it had run down her legs. Between that and the seepages from her vagina, she looked a sorry state indeed.

"Hey, Sarah. How's it going? Whatcha been up to? I guess I could put a TV in here or something to keep you occupied. Your face was on the news again tonight. I'm sure you'd love to see all the attention you're getting."

"Why don't you just kill me now and be done with it? You've had your fun, just get it over with."

Am I a Monster?

"Girlie, we ain't even gotten started yet. We got so much to do, so much to look forward to. I was in the pub just now. Everyone consoling me still about the poor kid's girlfriend still missing. I had to bite my tongue not to start laughing, you know. The poor schoolkid lost his girlie to some maniac, probably need counselling when they find her dead body. How about that? Me, counselling!"

"You're fucking sick, Andrew. Sick. I hope you catch fucking cancer and die slowly and horribly."

"Well, that's not a very nice thing to say, is it? After all I did for you. And how did you repay me? By humiliating me. Then trying to turn Karen against me. I think we need to wash your mouth out with soap. The rest of you too. You look and smell fucking disgusting."

"Not exactly my fault, is it?"

Andrew ignored her and left to run a bath among other things. He came back some ten minutes later and untied her wrist. "Well, let's get you bathed, shall we?"

He picked her up. She was much lighter than before. He could almost carry her with one arm. Careful not to put his hand where she was stained so as not to get it on himself, he carried her to the bathroom and held her over the top of the steaming bath. Then he dropped her in.

Her first reaction was to gasp loudly as she hit the water. Her eyes widened as did her mouth. It was a delayed reaction, the shock to her system too much for her to bare but as the boiling water covered her body she began to thrash wildly trying to get out. Andrew had not only filled the tub with boiling water instead of combining hot and cold, he'd also boiled the largest pot of water he could find. The water was beyond scalding. The pungent smell of bleach filled the room too, burning her wounds even more, the fumes blinding her.

Sarah flayed and scrabbled at the side of the bath

trying to get up, but Andrew punched her hard in the face and pushed her back down again. Already, her skin was a bright red, blisters beginning to form in several places. The skin around her crushed toes started to peel like old wallpaper. Steam filled the room. He thought he could hear her skin sizzling like bacon over her screams. The occasional splash of water landed on Andrew's arms causing him to wince and recoil. Yeah, that was fucking hot.

The air was taken quickly from her lungs as the water burned her skin. The hot steam running down her throat was probably burning her windpipe in the process. Andrew grabbed a long-handled brush he used for when a particularly messy shit required him to clean the inside of the toilet bowl. He grabbed hold of Sarah's hair which was already coming off in clumps and began to scrub her.

"Stay still, Sarah. I said you fucking stank, and we can't have you stinking the place up and alerting the neighbours, so the quicker you let me scrub you the quicker you can get out."

She was gasping now, incapable of speech, probably entering into shock, but the punch to the face had dulled her senses, weakened her even more than she already was. As Andrew scrubbed her arms and chest, great patches of skin came away, sticking to the tough hairs on the brush. Red, raw flesh was exposed underneath. Then, he lifted her up and turned her over, still holding onto her hair to prevent her from drowning. He scrubbed off all the shit on the back of her legs, scrubbed under her armpits, everywhere until she was clean again. She was moaning, possibly on the verge of falling unconscious, so Andrew dragged her from the bathtub and let her plop unceremoniously to the floor.

The water was filthy and grimy now. He thought of

Am I a Monster?

reaching in and pulling out the plug then decided against it. It could wait until the water was colder and he found some gloves to put on. Now that she was free from the water, she started to regain some semblance of consciousness, groaning and trying to crawl away. As she did more layers of skin were left behind as though shedding it. Blisters popped on her back, colourless secretions running down her sides like snot. She was bald in places now too. But now that she was clean once again, Andrew started getting an erection at the sight of her naked body.

He carried her back to the bedroom and was about to throw her back on the bed then remembered the sheets needed changing; bathing her would have been a complete waste of time if he let her roll around in her own filth again. Andrew dropped her on the floor, peeled off his own clothes and had sex with her where she lay. After he finished there was already another crimson leakage from her vagina.

Shaking badly, her eyes rolling around in her head, she then did something which shocked him, given her situation. She pushed herself up on her elbows and spat in his face.

Considering she must be in considerable pain, probably excruciating even, Andrew couldn't believe it. What must she be thinking? Right now, she should be begging to be freed, to be killed, anything to be put out of her misery, not challenging his authority once again. Andrew wiped the saliva from his face, took a step back and toe-punted her between the legs. She doubled over, now in a foetal position, groaning and panting heavily.

"You fucking bitch. The fuck do you think you are, huh? You're gonna fuckin' pay for that, you little whore."

He took another step back then kicked her in the

stomach, so hard she was kicked onto her other side. He kicked her in the back, on her backside, between the legs again. Andrew then grabbed a fistful of hair, pulled her up and punched her on the nose. He hit her so hard she fell down leaving Andrew with a clump of hair in his hand from where it had been torn out.

Sarah lay sprawled on the floor, bleeding from several places. His intentions after fucking her had been to give her something half decent to eat but now she could fucking starve for all he cared. He hated spitting, considered it a disgusting habit and this brought out all his rage whenever someone did it to him. If he didn't want to keep her and make her suffer more and for longer he might have killed her there and then. But instead, he grabbed her around the throat and brought her back up to his waist. Her eyelids were flickering, eyes barely open and she was moaning softly, blood running down her previously clean face, skin peeling everywhere. Andrew squeezed her cheeks together to force her mouth open then pissed down her throat.

Am I a Monster?

Chapter 13

There was always the possibility Sarah had been kidnapped by some sex-trafficking ring, black market organ suppliers, or just taken and raped by someone, the guy got scared and killed her, dumping her body somewhere. But Eric didn't think this to be the case. Such exotic options as sex traffickers or stealing organs was the kind of thing that happened in big cities, not close-knit villages like this one. Why would they come here to do their dirty work and risk being identified? In London there had to be thousands of kids sleeping rough on the streets that made their work so much easier. Yes, Bradwell and the surrounding villages had a dark history—more than most—but no one had ever been arrested for trafficking before or stealing organs, unless it was personal consumption. They were rapists, murderers, serial killers and worse, but not that. And if it had been someone that randomly picked up Sarah with the sole intention of raping her then getting the hell out, Eric was pretty sure they would have found the body by now.

There was a good chance the rapist had driven Sarah out to nearby Fritton Woods or the River Waveney that ran through it, and dumped her there, but helicopters, police dogs, and volunteers had scoured the whole area, divers included. It wasn't that dense an area for a body to remain undiscovered. A piece of clothing, anything. Therefore, the only logical conclusion Eric could come up with was that it had been someone from the village who took her. Someone who already knew her and Sarah had probably gone willingly with them. She might even be with them now, tied up somewhere. Whoever it was might have done so as a joke, a sick prank among kids and as soon as Sarah's face appeared on TV they had panicked, not knowing how to proceed. He refused to believe his little girl was dead. She would have put up one hell of a fight while defending herself and the kidnapper would be carrying the injuries to show it.

This was what he told himself and Tina anyway. That their girl was a fighter, she wouldn't give up without an almighty struggle, but the truth was, if he was honest with himself, he wasn't so sure. It seemed Sarah had always been the one the bullies picked on at school and she would come running home almost every afternoon bawling her eyes out. Because she was the odd one out, that liked to sit and read by herself instead of playing with the other girls. Because she was smaller than everyone else. Because it was so easy to taunt her, and she would crumble within seconds rather than retaliate or stand up for herself. Her mother didn't help, of course, mollycoddling the girl, telling her to just ignore them, tell the teachers, spoiling her. Eric had got the girl alone, sat with her and told her the more she cried and bawled and let them get away with it, the more they would do it. He never suggested she should fight back or lash out— as a police officer that was the last thing he could suggest although he often thought about it—but to stand up for herself. She was intelligent, all the books she read meant she must be able to come up with clever throwbacks to shut them up. Embarrass them enough they'd think twice rather than risk some witty and humiliating reply. But she couldn't do it, she said. When they called her names, instead of replying she would blush and crawl into herself like a tortoise, hiding within a shell. It pained and infuriated him, especially as he had always been the complete opposite, and now it seemed it had gotten the better of her. Only this time, her weakness might just

Am I a Monster?

cost her her life.

His mind was wandering. Understandable since he barely slept since Sarah went missing, patrolling the streets at night looking for her when he should be trying to rest and be there for Tina. But she was being comforted as best as possible by family members and neighbours, so he limited himself to the bare necessities when it came to sleeping. And more often than not, his sleep came in the form of a few hours here and there in his car, not wanting the claustrophobia of being surrounded by the family all day and night, fussing over them both.

He sat at a bar now, sipping a steaming mug of coffee early in the morning while the perpetually gloomy, grey clouds passed slowly and silently overhead. He couldn't remember the last time he'd seen the sun. It seemed to have disappeared along with his daughter, as though in a mark of respect. Kids hurried to school, the younger ones with their hands gripped firmly by mothers. Everyone knew now, of course, about Sarah and no parent wanted their child to be next should it be a serial criminal stalking the village. Only a few years ago there had been not one but two serial killers in nearby Belton, many children horrifically tortured and murdered. And one of them had been a detective—something that had shocked the nation. It may be why some parents and neighbours gave him sly looks as they passed him by on the streets, but he ignored them. It was perfectly understandable they were scared. He would be too if it was the other way round.

But maybe one of those parents was giving him the sly looks because they knew exactly where Sarah was. He didn't think so, though. Everything told him it had been someone around Sarah's age. She might be vulnerable and weak-minded at times but for those very reasons she would never go off with a stranger. If someone tried to drag her away someone would have seen something. Everyone saw something these days. Most of the news on TV was stuff people had recorded with their damn mobile phones. No, it had to have been someone from school, maybe even a teacher, and Eric had been an officer long enough not to believe in coincidences. The last person to see someone alive was usually the one that had caused such an event to happen in the first place.

As much as he tried though, the idea that Andrew was behind her kidnapping failed to gel in his head. The kid had seemed so genuinely shocked and horrified at Sarah going missing. It was true that it wouldn't be the first time someone had successfully tricked detectives and journalists with crocodile tears, fake despair and hollow pleading, but this was a kid. He would have to have a natural talent for acting and Eric wasn't prepared to believe that.

And yet, the instincts he had built up over the years, the cliché 'hunch' that many officers developed through their career, was not just a cliché seen in far too many movies—it was real. It had been proven time and time again. And what Eric's instincts were telling him was that there may be more to Andrew Foreman than he was letting on. The distance between where Andrew had left her and her home was too short, too many people in and around the area. If anyone had tried to bundle her into a car, at least one person would have spotted them. Someone who also knew Sarah. It was time to revisit Andrew again on his own, even though the task force had brought him back in for questioning recently. Ronald told him the kid had been a rock—impossible to get anything out of him so they had to remove him from their almost non-existent suspects list. Time to try again then.

Am I a Monster?

He quickly finished his coffee and hurried off towards the flat Andrew said he practically lived at these days. Hopefully, he'd catch him before he left for school. He arrived at eight-thirty and headed up to the flat, the entrance to the building open as usual. He knocked on the door and waited, listening carefully for any noises coming from inside. Eric knocked again, louder, and waited another ten minutes before disappointingly leaving. The kid must already be at school and not being directly on the task force he would not be allowed to remove him from class to speak with him. It was infuriating, but Ronald had made it very clear that he was not to get involved in any way that could jeopardise the case—he was too close. Bringing the boy in for questioning was down to the detectives and no one else.

So now what?

Easter was coming up soon and the schools would close this coming Friday anyway for the next two weeks and he knew that many in their last year of high school would not be averse to taking the odd day off until it was time for the exams. Shelly came across as one such person. He didn't know her very well, but he had occasionally overheard Sarah and Shelly chatting on the phone or in Sarah's room. It appeared that Shelly's immediate future revolved around having as much fun as possible and worrying about a career later. It had not started to rain so there was a very good chance Shelly had decided to stay at home today. Eric took out his notebook, found her address and went to her house instead.

The door opened after he knocked a couple of times and a dejected-looking Shelly stood there. When he'd spoken to her immediately after Sarah's disappearance, she had been both horrified and shocked to hear the news, unable to believe it. She had willingly told Eric and the detectives everything she knew about Sarah, their secret chats about boys they had crushes on, anyone who might have been bullying Sarah lately. But all Shelly could think of was Andrew and while there had been rumours about stuff he'd done when younger, that he might have something of a short temper, all the girls at school were infatuated with him and the boys looked up to him almost as a hero figure. Surely Andrew had nothing to do with it.

When pressed about these rumours, Shelly told the detectives and Eric that because he came from something of a broken home, he had been known to take out his frustrations on others, namely boys who had either said or done something he didn't like or find funny and had resorted to hitting back. One kid had his nose broken during a fight but that had been years ago. Andrew had been nothing but a cool kid since, she said, and no girls had any qualms about being his girlfriend. Shelly said she'd tried to set up a date with him many times but he wasn't interested. When Andrew had then taken an interest in Sarah, Shelly had been ecstatic for her, most of the other girls jealous. And as the days passed with still no sign of Sarah showing up, Shelly had changed from being the bubbly, outgoing girl to someone who looked like they needed urgent therapy, demanding to be informed of any and all news. To the point she became a regular visitor to the Greenwood household, offering and wanting to be with Tina and organising search parties at school during her free time. Maybe, just maybe, Shelly's sense of utter guilt and blaming herself for Sarah's disappearance meant she was holding something back. Maybe Sarah had been up to something Shelly hadn't wanted to reveal.

Her eyes widened when she saw Eric standing there, her long, brown hair dishevelled, wearing no makeup

Am I a Monster?

which was almost unheard of in teen girls these days and wearing her pyjamas. There were bags under her eyes which, for a sixteen-year-old, broke Eric's heart too. Sometimes he forgot Sarah had friends out there that were just as petrified and dejected as he was.

"You've got a lead? You found her?"

"No, Shelly, neither, I'm afraid. I was just hoping to speak with you again. No school today?"

"No, I...just don't feel like it. Nothing important happening today anyway."

"You shouldn't neglect school, you know. So hard to get a job these days as it is."

"I know but...I can't concentrate anyway. I feel I should be out there looking for Sarah instead. She is still alive, isn't she? I know she is, I feel it."

"Me too. But that's why I came over. Couple of things I was wondering about."

"Oh, sure, come in."

Eric stepped inside and Shelly led him to the living room and offered him a seat.

"You want coffee, tea? My parents are at work, but I make a pretty decent cup."

"No, I'm fine. Listen, between you and me, I refuse to accept that Sarah was taken by someone outside of the village. It had to be someone she knew and the last person to see her was Andrew. Nine times out of ten that usually end up being the person that orchestrated the disappearance, but unless he's a very good actor, nothing leads me to him. Is there anything that Sarah was involved with you haven't mentioned? Something embarrassing perhaps neither of you wanted me to know about? Or illegal, I don't know or care at this point anymore. You can trust me; I won't say anything to anyone."

Shelly shrugged her shoulders and resumed biting her

nails, whether from nervousness about giving away some confidential fact or not, he didn't know. She shook her head.

"There's nothing. Nothing that I didn't already tell you before. Sarah wasn't into anything illegal, doing stuff, didn't have secret boyfriends or anything. She was—is—too much of a plain Jane for all that. Sorry, by the way, but that's how she was. Preferring to stay at home and write her books instead of coming to parties with us. If anyone should have been taken it should have been me."

Shelly started sobbing. "If anyone deserved to get picked up and taken by some arsehole, I'm the one that deserved it, not her. I wish it was me, I really do. I'm sorry I can't be of any more use but there's really nothing about Andrew you don't already know. Yes, he had a bit of a dark side, but who doesn't? Especially given the upbringing he had. His dad beating him, his mother a drunk and rumours go around she prostitutes herself. People have seen men going in and out all the time. So yeah, he has a bit of a temper, doesn't like it when he loses control of the situation, but one can hardly blame him."

Eric's heart sank. This was not what he had been hoping to hear. He thanked Shelly, told her she could come over any time and left. Another dead-end. He stood leaning up against his car, unsure what to do. The frustration and impotence at knowing how to continue, what he could possibly do next was overwhelming. He was betraying his daughter's trust in him, both as a police officer and a father and it was killing him. Sarah, Tina, everyone would be expecting him to find his daughter yet he was clueless. A failure. So he did the only thing he could think of; he got in his car and drove randomly around the streets in the hope something

Am I a Monster?

clicked in his head.

And it did.

But not an idea or some clue he'd overlooked; it came in the form of Andrew strolling along the street. Eric pulled over and watched from a distance. Andrew was nowhere near his home or the flat he stayed at and obviously wasn't at school either. He was practically bouncing along the pavement, looking as though he was enjoying life and everything it had to offer. Eric found this curious. Andrew had phoned him several times since the first press conference asking for updates and always volunteered to help out with putting up missing person posters, joining in the search parties. He even got a group of friends, he said, and they scoured Fritton Woods looking for signs of her. He also said, like Shelly, that he felt as though it was his fault she was missing, if only he'd accompanied her home, none of this would have happened. But right now, Andrew didn't look like the grief-stricken boyfriend.

He got out of his car and followed him, keeping a good distance back on the other side of the busy main road. It was cold and wet now and Andrew had his hands in his pockets but the cold weather didn't appear to be dampening his spirits. From this distance, he wasn't sure, but he would swear Andrew was chuckling to himself. Then Andrew turned onto a side street. Eric quickly ran across the road and watched as the boy entered a block of flats. He followed after him. There were four floors in this building and evidently three flats on each floor. And when Eric checked the mailboxes inside, Andrew's surname was there but not his first name. Instead, it said Karl Foreman.

Why hadn't Andrew said anything about having a brother who owned his own flat? A rush of adrenaline prickled Eric's body. A dozen ideas ran through his mind and each concluded with entering that flat and finding his daughter tied and bound in there. His initial hunch about Andrew finally proven correct. Eric headed upstairs to the flat and knocked on the door, ready to fight or barge his way in if necessary. He continued knocking for several minutes but for the second time that day he received no answer. Either Andrew was avoiding him which was extremely suspicious or he had gone into someone's else's flat, maybe a friend's. Either way, Eric would be back again soon. Very soon.

He went back downstairs with the full intention of sitting outside the block of flats in the hope Andrew left again but as he headed down the stairs, a girl stopped suddenly upon seeing him. She looked to be about Sarah's age.

"Hey, you got a moment?" he asked.

She seemed dubitative, looking behind her as though debating whether to run.

"It's okay, just routine. Listen, you live here?"

"Err, no, a friend does. Why?"

"Do you know a kid called Andrew? Andrew Foreman?"

She stared at him for a while as if considering the question then shook her head. "Nope. Never heard of him."

"He would be about your age. Goes to Bradwell High School."

She continued shaking her head. "I told you, no. Don't I know you from somewhere?"

"You might have seen me on TV a week ago. What's your name, by the way?"

"Karen. Karen Winchester."

"Okay, Karen, my daughter is Sarah Greenwood. She was kidnapped last week, you must have heard about it."

"Oh. Oh, umm, yeah, I'm really sorry. I, err, gotta

Am I a Monster?

go."

She turned and began to hurry back outside as if something had spooked her.

"Hey, Karen! Wait! I just want to ask you a couple of questions."

But when Eric stepped foot outside, Karen was already gone.

J. Boote

Chapter 14

Karen was spooked. She thought she might have died of a heart attack at just sixteen-years-old. Her heart had leapt to her throat, choking her, trapped, when Sarah's father presented himself. She knew she recognised him from somewhere and yes, it sure as fuck had been on the TV. Him, his wife, and Andrew in the background, all with tears in their eyes, begging for the release of Sarah. She had been on her way to see Andrew because Dave wanted to borrow some game for the PlayStation and didn't have the courage to come himself. Not with Sarah there. She hadn't wanted to go herself, so to see the girl's father standing there, having somehow found out where Andrew lived was an utter shock. What if he got a search warrant? They kick the door in it would be all over and all of them going to prison forever. Despite the man's yells, she hadn't dared stop running until she made it back to Dave's.

It had taken Dave at least ten minutes for her to stop babbling and calm down and explain what was wrong. That had been an hour ago. As far as they knew Sarah was still alive; Andrew had been bragging the night before about hitting her then leaving her tied to the bed.

"We'll go to fucking prison, Dave. I knew we should never get involved but fuck. That fucking Andrew deserves to rot in hell and now he's implicated all of us in his sick games."

"Calm down, Karen, for fuck's sake. Over an hour has passed. If he had managed to get in the flat and find her, everyone would know about it by now. There'd be ambulances and cops and reporters everywhere but there ain't. I just went and looked remember. The old man

Am I a Monster?

must have knocked on the wrong door or somethin'. 'cause I seriously doubt Andrew would have let him in. We'll be all right but we better let Andrew know the girl's dad know where he lives. He must have been followin' him or somethin'."

"I guess so but I'm so fucking scared, Dave. I don't want to go to prison. I don't want to go back to that flat. I don't want nothing more to do with fucking Andrew or anything."

"I know, neither do I. But if we don't, he's liable to do the fuckin' same to us. He's a psycho. Honestly, the best thing that could happen is that he loses it and kills the girl. I don't want her to die, but if she's dead she can't escape and give our names. But if her dad knows where Andrew's flat is, it won't take long before he returns. I'm gonna phone him now and warn him."

He took out his phone and dialled Andrew's number. Karen listened, her heart in her throat again, unsure how Andrew's reaction might be. Even though Dave was sitting on his bed and Karen on a chair opposite, she could still hear Andrew screaming and hurling abuse. Andrew might get it in his head it was their fault or one of the others that were in on it. The kid was capable of anything especially if he lost control of any situation. Not being in control was what caused him to lose it and become so unpredictable. That, and not being the centre of attention in everything he did.

They'd both been at his house once and his mother was drunk, insulting him in front of Karen and Dave. Andrew's face had twisted into a menacing sneer. He kept telling her to shut the fuck up and when she wouldn't, he gripped her around the throat and lifted her off the floor, pinning her against the wall. After telling her for the last time to leave him the fuck alone he threw her across the room, her had slamming against the far wall. Apparently, she'd needed seven stitches in her head, such had been the force used. He laughed at her as she bled on the floor then spat in her face.

Dave finally hung up, having barely got a word in after explaining what happened and threw his phone on the bed in disgust.

"What? What'd he say?"

"He said he's out all day, got some shit to do and won't be back until later, but he was right pissed off. Said you must have led him there. I tried to tell him he was already there when you arrived, but he wasn't listenin'. Said he was gonna take it out on Sarah later and if he suspects we led the old man there, we better watch out."

"Fuck. Maybe we should make an anonymous call to the police or something. I tried to help Sarah last time I was there. I haven't told you or anyone but when you all came in and she was on the floor, it was because she kept begging me to let her go and in the end I did. But I told her, if Andrew comes in or catches her I'm denying everything. If you all had come in ten minutes later, she'd be free by now and she was only going to give Andrew's name.

"I'm really worried Andrew is going to do something bad to her. Like really bad. Worse than what he did to her feet. I think we should go there, take her some food at least. Andrew's out all day you said, so he won't catch us."

"No way, Karen, are you mad? First, we make an anonymous call, they can trace it. Second, all they gotta do is take samples from her and they'll have our DNA. We all fucked her, remember? I didn't want to but I'm not gonna say no in front of Andrew. And no way should we go to the flat. Let's just…try and keep out of his way and forget about Sarah. Whatever happens he's either

Am I a Monster?

gonna kill her regardless or beat the shit out of her. Her old man is probably watchin' the place anyway."

"Maybe, maybe not. He can't sit outside the place all day. If you don't want to, that's fine, but I'm going. I've still got the spare key he gave you. I'm going to take her some food, help clean her up a bit. At least then, should the worst happen, I can say I tried. I'll probably still go to hell but fuck it."

"Fuck. I knew you were gonna say that. Why'd you have to be so stubborn? Giving her somethin' to eat isn't gonna help her in the long run, Karen. Andrew'll probably kick it out of her when he gets back anyway."

"Probably, but at least my conscience will be semi-clear. You coming or not?"

"Fuck."

They arrived at the block of flats, taking a shortcut through an alley then scanning the streets nearby for any sign of Sarah's father. Once they were confident they were safe they quickly headed upstairs. Karen's nerves were so bad it took her three attempts to insert the key. They stepped inside, half expecting Andrew to be waiting for them, a large knife in his hands perhaps, as if somehow he'd guessed what they were up to and had been bluffing about being out all day. But the only person in the flat was Sarah, sprawled on the bed, half asleep. She recoiled when she heard them come in, no doubt assuming it was Andrew.

"Hey, Sarah, it's okay, relax. We're not here to hurt you. I won't ask how you feel because I can see. But look, Andrew's out all day so I thought to come over and bring you some food at least," said Karen.

Sarah eyed them both suspiciously. Maybe she thought they were playing with her as Andrew had done, leading her into a false sense of security. On their way, they'd stopped at a fast-food place and Karen had ordered a cheeseburger and Coke. She laid it on the bed and stepped back.

Sarah only had one arm tied to the bed, plus the padlock so she couldn't untie herself, and she looked seriously malnourished. Her body was covered in bruises and blisters that had popped leaving terrible scars and sores, her ribs starting to show as she slowly wasted away. There were bald patches on her head, her nose shattered and her face covered in dried blood. But the worst thing about her were her eyes. They reminded Karen of prisoner of war victims who had long given up any hope of rescue, just waiting to die and praying it came soon. Between Sarah's legs was a dried pool of blood too, also splashed onto her legs.

"What the fuck is he doing to you?" whispered Dave. He looked to be on the verge of tears. Karen already was.

Her hunger overriding any suspicions of a trick, Sarah stuffed the cheeseburger into her mouth. She sounded like a ravenous dog as she tore into it barely chewing it before swallowing. In three bites it was gone. Then she drank the Coca Cola in three long swigs and collapsed back onto the bed.

"Thank you. I appreciate it," said Sarah.

"It's okay. You know why we can't untie you, don't you? Andrew will kill us, but listen, your father was here earlier. He must have been following Andrew or something. I bumped into him as I was coming to get something. Look, it won't be long before they get a search warrant, or your father forces his way in. You'll be rescued. I swear that when it gets to court, we'll testify against him. He's a pig and a psycho; he deserves to spend the rest of his life in prison. The inmates doing to him what he's been doing to you. I'm sure it's a matter of hours before the police come knocking so hang in there." Karen brought out a tissue and wiped blood from

Am I a Monster?

Sarah's face.

"Really? It's not a prank. My dad really was here?"

"Yes! This morning. Maybe he knocked on the wrong door or something and left."

"I…I think I heard someone knocking. I can't remember. I don't know anything anymore. I think he burst my eardrums when he punched me last night. But listen, I think I started my period. It really hurts down there, and it's been bleeding a lot. I don't think it's just from where he kicked me either. But at least I'm not pregnant, right. Do you have anything?"

Dave turned away, looking sheepish and embarrassed. Karen fished in her bag and brought out a tampon and handed it to her. Sarah pushed herself up with considerable difficulty, groaning and wincing as she did so and gently eased the tampon in. She winced doing that too, which made Karen do the same. If just doing that caused her pain, what else had Andrew been doing to her?

Once inserted, Sarah lay back again on the bed. The slightest movement seemed to cause her some kind of discomfort. Karen was so tempted to break the restraint keeping her to the bed and letting her go and had to force herself not to. Self-preservation was key here. Karen was also a coward when it came to pain. She would have killed herself by now had she been in the same position.

"Listen, we better get going. Andrew won't be back until later, he said. With any luck your father will get that search warr—"

There was a knock on the door. Karen froze. Had she just talked up the police? If it was them and she opened the door, she was going to prison. And so was Dave. They both looked at each other, unsure what to do. The blood rushed from Dave's face—he looked like he'd seen a ghost. He crept over to the door. Karen tried to pull him back, but he ignored her. He peered through the spy hole in the door and visibly relaxed. Dave opened the door to Karen's horror.

"Hey, man, what are you doing here? Quick fuck behind Karen's bac—"

Rob slapped a hand over his mouth when he saw Karen standing there. He blushed, then grinned. "Oh, I get it. Threesome, eh? You dirty fuckers! Any room for me, that's why I came. Might as well use it while it's free, right!"

Rob was another disgusting figure in every sense of the word. Overweight, a constant ripe odour of sweat coming from his pores no matter how many times he showered and the same for his mop of curly, blonde hair—greasy within ten minutes of washing it. At sixteen his teeth were already yellowing, some having fallen out which suggested early gum disease. His laughter was a cackle which at first might have been amusing but soon become an eternal nuisance. He was another that came from a poor, neglected background and as a result, the clothes he wore were often dirty and smelly from lack of washing. He would often wear the same clothes all week and there were suspicions the same could be said of his underwear and socks. Most of the time people smelled Rob's arrival rather than saw or heard him. As a result, he had few friends, one of them being Andrew who he looked up to as a godly figure. Dave and Karen both agreed that Andrew allowed him into his small circle of friends so he could exercise complete control over him, which he did. If Andrew asked Rob to set himself on fire and jump out a window, he would.

He was also quite sadistic. Until Sarah came along, he was thought to be a virgin. He always seemed quite happy not to have a girlfriend, knowing full well his own undesirable qualities, but this didn't stop him pinching

Am I a Monster?

the girls' breasts or backsides on occasions, often resulting in being called to the headmaster's office at school. He'd even been suspended twice for attempting to drag a girl into the boy's toilets. So for Rob, having Sarah here tied and bound was like a gift from God. Andrew had told him he could come around any time he pleased if he wanted to fuck Sarah.

Karen was horrified. If she said she and Dave were here for anything than taking advantage of Sarah, Rob would go running to Andrew and tell him, but neither of them wanted anything more to do with the torture and rape of Sarah. Now though, it seemed they didn't have a choice in playing along.

"Andrew asked us to keep an eye on her," said Karen. "He's out all day so we just popped in to make sure she wasn't trying to escape or scream for help."

"Yeah, I believe ya," said Rob, winking slyly. "Well, I came here 'cause I was bored. Fancied a quick blowjob. But seeing as we're all here, we could, you know, take turns or somethin' if you want. I don't mind. I can wait, I got all day."

He waddled over to Sarah and twisted her nipples as though tuning a radio. She groaned and tried to turn over onto her back. When she did, Rob squeezed her buttocks hard then slapped them.

"I get it, you want it up the arse, do ya? Dirty bitch. I see Andrew's got her well trained already. Bit tired today though, maybe tomorrow. So, Dave, you want firsts or seconds?"

"Err, excuse me, but my boyfriend already has a girlfriend, thank you."

"Ah, right, shit, yeah got it. Okay, so you gonna stand there and watch? I don't care either way."

"No, we're not gonna stand and watch, Rob. We're not pervs."

"You didn't seem to mind when we gangbanged her the other day. Oh well."

Dave and Karen left the room while Rob unzipped his trousers and gripped Sarah around the throat. They could hear her gagging and choking, Rob wheezing as he violated her. After a few seconds they heard him groan, followed by him zipping up his trousers again.

"Phew, that was quick. You can come back in again, I'm done."

Dave and Karen returned to the room. Sarah was vomiting up the hamburger she'd eaten earlier while replacing the bloodied tampon Rob must have pulled out before. Rob lit a cigarette, completely indifferent to Sarah's suffering. In fact, he was chuckling as he watched her.

"Well, that was fun, but now I'm bored. What shall we do now?"

Dave and Karen looked at each other. "Well, we really need to get going. I promised my mum I'd help with stuff at home," said Karen.

"What? That's boring, fuck that. Wait, I know! I saw this thing the other day that was super cool."

He pulled a knife out from his back pocket. Karen's heart missed a beat. Rob was not averse to threatening people if necessary if he didn't like their jokes.

"Hey, Rob, look, put that away, we really do need to get outta here. Let's go."

"Nah, wait. Ever since I saw it, I always wanted to try it. Watch."

He took a final drag from his cigarette and stubbed it out by shoving it up Sarah's backside. She screamed and buckled as he forced it all the way. The cigarette hissed as it went out. Then, he straddled her as she lay on her back groaning and began to carve into her skin. When he finished, he grinned and looked back at them. He'd made

Am I a Monster?

some kind of diagram.

"Okay, I'll go first. You know how to play noughts and crosses, right?"

In one of the squares he'd made, he sliced a cross then handed the knife to Karen. "Your turn."

Blood ran down Sarah's sides, soaking the filthy, stained bed. Every time Rob cut into her, she spasmed and tried to scream but was too weak. He used Sarah's top to wipe the blood from the diagram so they could see the squares. Karen flinched. She had no choice but to play along, or Rob would get suspicious. Andrew already mistrusted her; she knew from the way he looked at her sometimes. Karen took the knife and cut a circle into another square.

"Ooh, that's crafty. Okay, try this."

Karen winced and had to force herself to look at what she was doing as she played his game. Dave looked like he wanted to throw up. That, or kick the shit out of Rob. Finally, the game was over. Karen was the winner. It appeared as though someone had tried their hand at tattooing for the first time and seriously messed up. Sarah's whole back was a mess of circles and squares, some of the incisions made into her back deep.

"Fuck, you beat me. All right, your turn, Dave. You ain't beating me as well."

Rob started this time on one of her buttocks. And once again lost.

###

Rob didn't like losing. Especially to a girl. It made him feel insecure, weak. He was insecure enough as it was given his tendencies to sweat a lot, the acne on his face, his obesity. His parents had tried to get him to take more care of himself, perhaps join the school football team or the gym to keep his weight under control, but he always refused. Just jogging a few metres caused the sweat to drip down his sides and forehead. Followed by a constant, rancid odour that clung to him like a shroud. He was perfectly aware everyone taunted him behind his back, but fortunately for them, no one dared do it to his face. Or there would be serious consequences. The only one that didn't laugh at him was his mate, Andrew. A good kid. There should be more like him, he always said.

Dave and his stupid girlfriend had already left him alone with a groaning, whimpering Sarah. She probably laughed at him too. When she wasn't crying, of course. And he made damn sure she did that a lot. Like now. Whenever Rob's feelings of inadequacy reached maximum levels, to the point he sometimes wished he was dead, after an initial sense of despair and sorry, it would be replaced by rage and frustration. The need to punch something, someone, anything to unleash all that pent-up anger. Usually, it was his younger brother who paid the price, but not anymore. Now, he had his very own punchbag and it was something he was determined to make the very most of.

He rolled her over onto her back and glared at her face. She had been pretty once. Would have made a good girlfriend to someone. Even had the intelligence to go with it. A fucking published author at sixteen. Rob could barely read let alone write. It pissed him off how some people had everything while others, like him, had nothing. She didn't deserve to have more than him. Why should she? She should have nothing as well. It gave him an idea.

He found what he was looking for in one of the cupboards and returned to find Sarah barely conscious. He sat beside her on the bed and slapped her hard across the face then prodded her broken nose. Fresh blood began to dribble down her cheeks.

"Think you had it all, eh? Yer fuckin' books and

Am I a Monster?

pretty face. Bet you think you're fuckin' better'n everyone else. Well, yer wrong. Time we finish with you, people'll think yer a fuckin' freak. Belong at the circus. And even then…Bitch."

He raised the pliers and brought them down hard onto her teeth trying to knock them out. It was obvious Sarah took good care of them too because they barely moved. Three times he smashed the pliers into her mouth destroying her once full lips in the process but all he had achieved was to dislodge a couple of molars. A rancid smell rose from the bed and at first he assumed it was his sweat until he saw the growing wet patch beneath Sarah. Now more annoyed than ever, he forced the pliers into her mouth, gripped a front tooth and wrenched as hard as he could. But still it wouldn't move.

He gripped the pliers with both hands and began tugging back and forth so her whole head was brought up off the blanket and slammed back down again. Finally, the tooth started wiggling. He twisted the pliers left and right until the tooth broke in half and came away. Then he repeated the process with a molar. This one came away easier, leaving the nerve exposed. When he touched it with the tip of the pliers, Sarah's body jerked violently.

"Painful, huh?"

Rob pulled two more molars from her mouth until the exertion left him feeling tired and sweaty and hungry. He tied the now unconscious girl to the bed and headed home, happy with his day's work. A Big Mac was called for to celebrate then probably a good session in front of the computer watching Pornhub.

Chapter 15

"Hey, you!"

Andrew momentarily froze, convinced it was Sarah's father or a detective. The game was up, he'd been caught before he could finish it. But when he turned it was a woman standing there, someone he vaguely recognised. Then it hit him—the neighbour from below, Jackie or something.

"Yeah, what?"

He barely spoke to her or any of the neighbours because he liked to keep to himself and now he certainly didn't want any of them getting too friendly and deciding to pay a visit. The way she called his name though did not suggest a friendly chat.

"You really need to keep the noise down up there or I'm gonna have to call the police. I don't want to, and I know you've been through a lot of shit lately, but you can't be yellin' and shoutin' all day and night.

"I don't know who you got in there but the girl sounded like she was goin' through hell. And you, you wanna be careful, police are gonna think you did somethin' to that girlfriend of yours. I know you didn't but tell them that."

Andrew was shocked. He'd been out all day and as far as he knew no one had been to his flat. The day before Rob had phoned him to tell him about his game with Dave and Karen, but today no one had come. It had been a quiet day, Sarah semi-conscious from the beating he gave her before he left, stubbing out his cigarette on her tongue to keep her quiet. Or so he thought. He'd had sex with her after admiring the bloody scars on her back and buttocks and had kicked her a few times after she

Am I a Monster?

complained, several times to the head, shattering her nose for the third time. So how the fuck had she found the strength to start screaming?

"Sorry. It was just me and a friend, she got a little drunk and was messing about. I was out all day yesterday helping with the search party and well, earlier I was a little depressed again. Sarah's out there somewhere, I know it, but sometimes it gets too much. Won't happen again."

"I know, and that's why I didn't wanna call the police, but…you ain't helping Sarah by getting drunk and raucous."

"Yeah, you're right. Sorry."

He left before she could continue the conversation. He arrived at the flat, let himself in and locked it behind him. He immediately went to the spare bedroom where Sarah lay on the bloodstained bed. Andrew stood there for a while glaring at her. She stared back, one eye almost closed and a yellow-purple colour around the edge from where he'd punched her.

"What am I gonna do with you, Sarah? Huh? I thought we had an understanding that you were gonna do as you're told. That if you tried to call for help or escape, it was only going to make matters worse."

He tutted and shook his head. What was it with people nowadays? All they had to do was what they were told and life would be so much easier, but no. He was losing control here and this was not the way things were supposed to be. Control was important. Control over others and everything was what helped Andrew retain a semblance of order, of purpose. When Dave had phoned him to tell him Sarah's father had discovered his location he had been tempted to rush back and beat the pair of them to shit too. There was no way he could have followed Andrew, he had been so careful to ensure he wasn't followed or spotted, so it had to be someone else. Apparently, it had been Karen who Eric had confronted.

Karen.

Again.

Her girly instincts were getting the better of her, feeling sorry for Sarah, girl to girl. He was going to have to do something about her too and soon. When he got home last night he had been so tempted to go to her house and drag her here, tie her to the bed and make her understand what she was doing wrong. But that would have brought problems and those he had enough of already. Problems caused stress and stress led to mistakes. And for the first time in his sad, pathetic life he had control over Sarah and the others. All of them now had to do exactly as he said or they would all suffer equally. Either by dying or going to prison the rest of their lives. It had been so easy taking Sarah then involve his so-called friends. He knew they wouldn't be able to resist free sex, someone to take their frustrations out on, just like him. And Karen was too smitten with Dave to say or do anything that might get him in trouble.

And now, not only was Karen betraying their trust, Sarah was misbehaving too. He was losing control and fast.

"Things are going to change around here, Sarah. A lot. For one thing, if you're going to be living here with me, you need to pull your weight. This place is a shithole so you can start by doing a few chores. I'm sure you can walk more or less properly by now; your toes are getting better already. Not so purple and bruised anymore.

"I'll have to keep the door locked, of course, maybe ask Rob to pop over when I'm not here to keep an eye on you. Put locks on the windows too, but I don't think you're gonna make the same mistake twice, are you?"

"I…I don't know what you're talking about, Andrew.

Am I a Monster?

I didn't scream or anything. I'm too tired, too weak. You saw what your friends did to me yesterday. My back is killing me. I can barely move anyway."

Andrew's patience was waning fast. Why did people have to lie so blatantly in others' faces? He had proof she'd been screaming and shouting—he just told her. Sarah evidently didn't understand or appreciate the gravity of the situation she found herself in. He leaned in closer and gripped what remained of her hair then spun her around and raked his fingernails down her back, splitting open the wounds again. Fresh blood ran down pooling on the bed. Sarah screamed. Now that she was covered in bruises and scars and dried blood everywhere he didn't even find her attractive anymore. The idea of having sex with this ravished, filthy, stinking thing repulsed him. The others could do what they liked with her, but he didn't want anything more to do with her sexually. He threw her back on the bed and lit a cigarette, thinking how he might punish her. She looked like an old crone now, wasting away, but it was her own fault. It was for the best.

Then he saw it.

His body started shaking with fury. That fucking bitch hadn't been here with Rob and Dave looking to have a bit of fun at Sarah's expense. Karen was betraying him, everyone, going behind his back, questioning his authority in his own fucking home. Andrew took a final drag on his cigarette and stubbed it out on Sarah's nipple. Then he brought out his lighter and with one foot kicked Sarah's legs apart so she was spreadeagled on the bed.

"So not only have you been trying to draw attention to yourself, screamin' and shoutin' for help, you've been gettin' that help, haven't you?"

Sarah was sobbing, trying to curl into a ball but Andrew wouldn't let her. Instead, he set fire to the piece of string dangling from her vagina. As though suddenly awakened Sarah writhed and screamed desperately trying to remove the burning tampon, but Andrew flicked her arm away and watched as the flame reached the lips of her vagina. She buckled and thrashed but it was no good—she wasn't going anywhere. Eventually, the flame died out but not before leaving large blisters on the affected area, that popped and seeped colourless secretions. Whether the flames had entered her body or not and set fire to the contraption within, he didn't know, only that the stench of burning flesh was terrible. As a bonus, he took out his lighter again and melted her clitoris. Sarah was such a whore she probably enjoyed the gangbangs from the others. Not anymore, though. As Sarah's screams intensified, he went and opened a window.

"I'm off out to get something to eat, but when I come back, you can start pulling your weight around here. Place looks like a fucking pigsty."

Chapter 16

Even though he should know better, Eric made a habit of visiting Ronald's office every afternoon when he arrived to start his shift. His boss had asked him if he wanted to change to the morning shift, but he said no. He didn't tell his boss, but he liked to patrol the streets at night in the vague hope of seeing his daughter somewhere, maybe abandoned by her captor. Or to see the kidnappers lurking around trying to find another victim, drug dealers who might have seen or heard something. He made it quite clear to the dealers he knew that he couldn't care less right now about what they got up to, if they promised to keep an ear and an eye on the shady underworld. If anyone was going to hear anything useful, it would be those that already lurked there.

According to Ronald, every single sex offender, murderer, armed robber, anyone who had been convicted of serious crimes in the last ten years had been interviewed. Over two thousand just in the surrounding villages and the small town nearby, Yarmouth. Eleven hundred homes had been searched, mostly from anonymous tips from neighbours, all of which proved to be false leads. Ten times search parties had been set up, both officially by the police and also by locals, checking every area of wasteland, parks, out at Fritton Woods where even the farmers had joined in, roaming the fields in their tractors and with dogs. A reward for information leading to the discovery of Sarah had first been set at two thousand Euros and two days ago, after speaking with the bank and re-mortgaging his house, Eric had raised it to twenty-five thousand Euros. Almost three thousand posters had been taped to the walls and lamp posts around Bradwell. And still no one came forward.

Tina was on the verge of a nervous breakdown. She'd lost so much weight in the last two weeks, none of her clothes fit her anymore. Tina's sister, Margaret, virtually lived with them now, sleeping with Tina while Eric was out at work, Eric himself sleeping in the spare bedroom. Tina barely ate and what she did she almost invariably vomited it back up again later. Privately, their doctor told Eric he was extremely worried about her and the suggestion of a few days at Northgate Hospital for the Mentally Impaired had been made. Eric dismissed it immediately, knowing Tina would refuse in case her daughter turned up. It was something that hung in the air between them, like a ghost, flitting back and forth during the few moments they spoke, but neither dare pronounce the fatal words. '*Our daughter is gone forever*'. Neither came out and said it but they could both sense it in each other. The forbidden words no one was allowed to utter unless it came with proof. Once again, that traitorous feeling of hope was both a blessing and a curse.

There was another phrase which tore just as many holes in Eric's heart.

"We're at a dead end."

This and similar phrases had been repeated to Eric several times over the last few days whenever he visited Ronald's office. It was becoming a cold case, no further leads, no more anonymous tips. The phone has stopped ringing. All saying exactly the same thing—that unless someone happened to stumble over a dead body somewhere, Sarah wasn't coming home. This wasn't London either, with unlimited resources. Sarah's missing body wasn't the only case detectives had to work on. The criminal activity didn't go on hiatus just because a girl was missing. It meant that with no leads they were forced to turn their attention to other areas.

Am I a Monster?

Eric was practically a one-man band when it came to hunting down Sarah.

And all his focus was still centred on a sixteen-year-old boy who had also helped in every single search party and putting up missing person posters around the village. But Eric was not entirely convinced still. Especially given his conveniently failing to mention he had his own flat. Could it have been a decoy saying he spent his time at a friend's flat so as not to give Eric his real address? Eric thought it might.

He sat outside now as he had been doing all morning before going home. It was a Saturday which meant no school so there was a good chance Andrew would be asleep. Since discovering the flat, Eric had made it his business to watch the place a lot. His first thought had been to run to Ronald and demand they request a search warrant, but at the same time he didn't want to spook Andrew. It was also his last hope; if Sarah wasn't here, she wasn't anywhere. The willpower necessary to stop himself from running to Ronald was immense. Sarah could be dying right this very moment. He would never forgive himself if they found her a fraction too late, but he also wanted to catch her kidnapper by his own hand. He would be taking care of things himself first before handing over her kidnapper, but the question kept returning—what if?

Then it happened again. Just like before, he was about to go home, defeated, when he saw Andrew practically bouncing along the street seemingly without a care in the world. This was not a kid desperate to find the whereabouts of a loved girlfriend. And strangely enough, whenever he passed a neighbour or someone who evidently knew him, his demeanour changed completely. From his vantage point, Eric could see the grin suddenly disappear, his head now hung low, a pat on the back from the neighbour and Andrew wiping his eyes. The second the neighbour passed by Andrew raised his head again, smiling to himself.

It was one of the most difficult moments of Eric's life. He was torn. Follow the kid to his flat and barge in, check for himself, or go tell Ronald he suspected Andrew of misleading them all? If he did indeed force his way in and Sarah wasn't there, Andrew could press charges, but more importantly, he would know Eric was suspicious of him still. Better to do things the right way. It was, after all, his daughter's life what mattered, not personal vengeance and gain. Eric started the engine and drove to the station.

Three hours later, Eric was stunned. He had to sit down before his legs betrayed him. Despite everything Ronald told the judge and Eric's suspicions, the judge denied them a search warrant based on lack of evidence or not enough reason to warrant it. Eric had wanted to speak to the judge himself, but Ronald refused. The judge had only listened to Ronald on a Saturday because Sarah's life might be in danger; otherwise, he would have had to wait until Monday.

"But this is my daughter we're talking about! She could be in danger and Andrew's behaviour does not concur with how one would expect a grieving boyfriend to act. Let's just go to the fucking flat now and demand he let us in."

"We can't, Eric. He could sue us for harassment if she's not there. Honestly, I'm as shocked as you are. We've got nothing else to go on but this could screw up everything. All we can do is put surveillance on him and hope he fucks up. Starting immediately by the way. If Sarah is in there, we'll find her. I'll have detectives watching the place all day and night."

It wasn't enough. He had visions of finding Sarah's

Am I a Monster?

dead body in Andrew's flat and the coroner telling him she had died right around the time they had requested a search warrant. Tina would never look at him again. He'd never be able to sleep at night knowing that saving her had been in his grasp. It was all very well putting surveillance on Andrew, but it could be too late. There was a precedent here. The girl, Sophie, saved from her kidnapper, a rogue detective, who had kept her in a secret room in his basement and whose intentions had been to gradually slice off parts of her body to eat until there was nothing left. The detective found his daughter after sneaking into the house one night and hearing muffled sobs in the basement. Long strips of flesh were missing from her arm as was one of her organs, crudely removed then the stomach stitched up again. Sophie had gone into shock and had been in a coma for two weeks before finally, inevitably, she had died from her injuries. If the judge wasn't going to issue a warrant, he decided there and then he'd issue his own. He and Andrew were, after all, friends now, united in a common goal to find Sarah.

Eric muttered an insult about the judge to Ronald and headed out, straight to Andrew's flat.

He double checked to make sure he got the right floor and flat number right and climbed the stairs. A couple of people walked past him, glaring at him in his police uniform then turning back for a second glance. They probably recognised him from the TV—he'd gone on air again only the day before pleading for information. Eric ignored them. He found the flat and knocked on the door, straining to hear any sounds inside. He thought he heard shuffling but when no one came to answer he knocked again, his ear pressed against the door. There was a thud, he was sure of it, then footsteps. Eric stepped back, for reasons he wasn't entirely sure why, his body tense, ready to fight.

The door opened and Andrew stood there, looking neither surprised or shocked. "Mr Greenwood, hi."

Nothing about how he found him, no look of horror at being discovered. It was as if he'd been expecting him.

"Hello, Andrew. Not surprised to see I know where you live? Apart from that other flat with your friends?"

"Well, no. I assumed you already knew. This is my brother's flat, he lives in London but pretty much left it to me. I come over now and again to clean it up and open the windows a bit. It's why I'm here now. No school today and I was going to go with friends back out to Fritton later, to continue searching for your daughter."

But Eric was barely listening. He was looking over Andrew's shoulder into the flat for any signs of his daughter. But he heard nor saw anything to indicate she might be here.

"That right? Any chance I could come in? I could use a toilet. Been out patrolling all night and I think my bladder is gonna burst."

"Oh, umm, sure."

Andrew stepped aside and let Eric in. All Eric's senses were on high alert. All his police training and what to look for in a similar situation came into play. He stepped into the living room, the place a mess with empty beer cans everywhere, ashtrays overflowing, the carpet filthy and stained. His eyes roved everywhere, every corner, even the ceiling. His nostrils flared, searching the unmistakable odour of blood, perhaps even Sarah's favourite perfume that she'd been wearing the day she disappeared. Yet despite the filthy aspect the flat provided—which he guessed was normal for a teen kid anyway—there was no indication of Sarah's presence. But that didn't mean she wasn't or hadn't been here.

"So, the toilet is just down the hall on the left," said Andrew. "As I said, the place is a bit of a mess. A

Am I a Monster?

friend's birthday last night so we came here to celebrate. As you can see."

"That right?"

He left Andrew standing there and headed down the hall. It was a small flat, more a bachelor's pad Eric thought as he purposefully entered a room on his right. He quickly scoured the room—Andrew's bedroom judging from the posters on the wall and another overflowing ashtray by the bed—then left and entered another bedroom to his left. Something seemed off about this room. The bed was unmade, missing its sheets, blanket and pillow but there was a stain on the bed, a dark colour. The window was wide open, a stiff breeze blowing into the room, but he was sure he caught the pungent odour of urine or something similar to ammonia. There were a lot of dark stains on the light-brown carpet too, as if this room had been used recently and Andrew had decided to hastily remove the bed sheets. He hadn't heard any washing machine spinning when he came in though. Otherwise, the room was completely bare, not even a wardrobe in here, which made him wonder what the room had been used for. Maybe one of his friends last night had crashed in here and had thrown up in bed—again, perfectly normal for kids having a party. But when he put a hand on the bed, it was warm, so whoever had been sleeping here had got up recently. He thought of the people who'd passed him on the stairs, but one was a young couple, another a middle-aged man, not the type who Eric expected to be here. And besides, what was Andrew doing throwing parties if he was supposed to be grieving the disappearance of his girlfriend?

Eric decided to look under the bed. Something was off with this room, smelling completely different to the rest of the flat.

"Wrong room," said Andrew suddenly, causing Eric to jump. He'd been so focused on looking for signs of Sarah he'd forgotten Andrew was even here.

"Oh, sorry, my mistake. Someone fall asleep in here, did they? Little too much to drink and mess your bed?"

"Yeah, my friend's girlfriend. I have the sheets in the washing machine now. She's not used to drinking, I guess. I think she wet herself too."

"Happens, I guess."

Eric left the room, casting one last look at the bed before heading to the toilet. He pretended to take a leak then left, to find Andrew waiting for him at the bottom of the hallway.

"That's better, thanks. You know, I might come with you folks later out to Fritton. I…I just…"

"I'm so terribly sorry, Mr Greenwood. I can't stop thinking about her. You know, if I ever get my hands on whoever did this…well, I don't think the police will be involved. And you know what, I don't care if I spend the rest of my life in prison; it will be worth it."

Eric thought about that for a few seconds, how he was so convinced he'd finally found his daughter and sobbed on Andrew's shoulder.

###

Tina almost jumped from the sofa where she spent most of her time, eyes expectant as always despite having lost all sparkle in them.

"Anything? You find anything?"

Eric had told her about discovering Andrew's flat and she had somehow found renewed hope, something that died inside her days ago. It had to be where Andrew was keeping her and her husband had once again saved the family. Andrew would be brought to justice, her beloved daughter soon home with her. She knew it had to have been that kid. Ever since Sarah came running in that

Am I a Monster?

Friday night, eyes puffy and glazed, her suspicions had been proven. Andrew had probably drunk too much and his stinking hands had tried to delve where they shouldn't. Sarah had foolishly agreed to meet him again and the kid had taken her. What he had been doing to her all this time, she refused to contemplate.

Then Tina saw the look of despair on Eric's own face. He didn't need to say anything. It was clear the answer.

She sank back onto the sofa in utter shock. She had been so confident Eric would find the girl there. How can he not have?

"W…What do you mean, no? She's not there? Tell me you found her. Alive. It's okay, if she's at the hospital or something and…and bad, it's okay, just tell me. I need to know she's at least alive."

"She wasn't there, Tina. I searched the whole flat. No sign of her at all."

She stared at him for a few seconds, waiting for a smile to appear on his face and to rush over and hug her. A morbid joke he'd just played on her. She was fine, at the hospital for a check-up, just in case, but alive and well, Andrew already in custody. But instead of that happening, Eric came and slumped beside her, then brought her into his arms.

She pushed him away, on the verge of hysterics. For the last week, she barely had the strength for anything. Every time her sister, now asleep upstairs, tried to make her eat, she would promptly vomit it back up again, her nerves betraying her. It was as though she was living in a cloud, a nightmare, everything fuzzy and hazy around her. Despite taking sleeping tablets they made no difference. She would wake up screaming in the middle of the night in a cold sweat, having dreamt of stumbling across Sarah's body being eaten by rodents and foxes while lying in some festering ditch somewhere. During the day, every time someone came down the garden path, she was convinced it was a detective coming to tell her he was very sorry, but they had just found what was left of Sarah's remains under a hedge. They would need her to come and identify the body because it was so badly mutilated. She imagined Andrew doing despicable things to her. Eric had wanted to bring the kid home for dinner, saying he felt sorry for him, surely innocent. It was Tina that refused to have him in her home.

"Whadaya mean, she isn't there? What kind of a father and cop are you that you can't even find your own fucking daughter!" she spat. "You didn't look hard enough, she *has* to be there! Go check again. Take the task force people with you. Don't you dare come home and tell me my daughter wasn't there!"

She burst out crying, energy depleted with her outburst. Eric said nothing.

"Where's my baby, Eric? Someone just please tell me where she is. I can't go on anymore like this. Take me instead of her."

Tina curled up on the sofa and cried until she fell asleep.

Chapter 17

It was too easy. Really, when one thought about it, keeping calm, maintaining control over complicated situations, using's one head and not panicking made everything so much easier. Take the time to think things through and all problems will solve themselves. It was what Andrew told himself when he looked through the spy hole and saw Eric standing there. He already knew the man had discovered where his flat was, but he hadn't expected him to turn up unannounced. Occasionally, they would text each other, keep each other updated on any leads that might have surfaced, so the fact he appeared at his flat without any warning could only mean one thing. He was suspicious.

Andrew had tried to be careful about how he acted in public, but he also knew he would always be on the suspect list no matter what he said and did—it was the law of averages as far as the police were concerned—but even so, to see the man still suspecting him after all this time was something of a shock. Regardless, Andrew had been quick to run to Sarah's room, throw open a window to remove the nasty smells, then gag and tie Sarah underneath the bed, removing all the bedsheets in the process. He just had enough time to throw them in the washing machine before Eric banged on the door again. Then, as if that wasn't enough the old fuck had tried to be clever and gone searching in all the rooms as Andrew knew he would. The man thought Andrew had Sarah kidnapped in here and wanted to locate her on his own. It made him wonder why they hadn't got a search warrant and he could only assume they didn't have enough evidence, so Eric had been forced to use alternative methods to get in. Well now the joke was on him. Eric had come within touching distance of his daughter, but he might as well have been miles away.

Sarah had been too weak to alert her father anyway which was another stroke of luck on his behalf. When he dragged her out and threw her back on the bed, he wasn't sure she was even aware of how close rescue had been. He stood over her wretched body now. It wasn't going to do her any good pretending to be too weak and ill to do her part around the flat either. If she was going to be living here with him, she had responsibilities. And they were going to start right now.

"Hey, Sarah, wake up!" he yelled, slapping her face.

The girl looked emaciated. With most of her hair missing, she might have resembled someone in advanced stages of some terminal disease. Her broken nose was twisted in two places and hooked that reminded him of an old hag. Bruises covered her whole body, her private parts as though she had some terrible sexual disease with broken blisters around where he'd set fire to the tampon and clitoris, still inside her as far as he knew. Her toes were turning black, terribly swollen so it was hard to determine which was her big toe and little toe. Her nipples were red raw from where he and Rob had twisted them. The scars on her back and buttocks continued leaking blood and pus too—to the point there was a very good possibility they were now infected and the pain must have been intense because she couldn't stand up straight—hobbling about bent over like an old lady. In another time she might have been considered a leper.

She was pathetic. He slapped her again, then tugged on her broken toes, twisted her nipples once more, flicked her broken nose, toying with her. As though caressing her he ran a finger over her clitoris, then

Am I a Monster?

pressed down hard. Sarah arched her back in agony which subsequently opened the wounds there even more.

"C'mon, Sarah, time to get to work. This place is a shithole, and you're not living here rent-free. Get up."

She groaned and tried to curl up, so Andrew gripped her around the neck and threw her to the floor. He kicked her in the stomach. Finally, she opened her eyes.

"Please, please stop. Just kill me if you want, I don't care anymore. Why are you doing this to me?"

"Because you asked for it. We've been over this a dozen times already. Get up."

She tried to push herself up but collapsed again.

"For fuck's sake."

Andrew squatted and dragged her up. She swayed on her feet, grimacing, eyeballs rolling in her head. He dared to let go, expecting her to fall down again, but she didn't which was a pleasant surprise.

"Good, now, I think you should start in the living room. The boys will be coming over soon, and I don't want them to think we're lazy here. I want you to gather up all the crap, throw it away then hoover the floor. After that, you can start in the kitchen. Go."

Almost zombie-like, Sarah shuffled off, her knees buckling on occasions. If she did a good job, he decided he might give her a sandwich or something. He couldn't remember the last time she'd eaten, which reminded him he was hungry himself. He accompanied Sarah into the living room, explained where the rubbish bags were and everything else she might need, then went to make himself some toast.

"Oh," he said, before leaving her, "if you try anything funny, like escaping or screaming, I will cut your hands off remember. One finger at a time. Now get to fucking work." He left her cleaning while he went and played on the PlayStation for a while.

Thirty minutes he gave her, more than enough time to finish her chores, so when he went back into the living room and found her sprawled on the sofa asleep, still with chores to do, he was not happy.

"I get it, slacking on the job your first day. I can see you're not quite convinced about how serious I am. All right, don't say I didn't warn you." He went and fetched his toolbox.

She was still sprawled there when he got back, completely ignoring his threats. He put the toolbox on the table and brought out a hammer and two four-inch nails.

"I warned you, Sarah, I really did. All you had to do is what you're told. It's the basis for every happy family. Follow the rules, do as you're told. It's really quite simple. Control, Sarah, it's not rocket science."

"Just leave me alone."

"Nope."

Andrew straddled her as she lay on her back. He took one nail and with the hammer punched the nail through her left nipple. That woke her from her lethargy as the nail entered her breast. She convulsed and screamed, trying to buckle Andrew off her but she was too weak. He continued until the nail was hammered in completely. Then he repeated the process with her other nipple. When he finished, he sat back to admire his work. It took piercing to a whole new level. It occurred to him that if put two magnets on the nail heads, he could use her breasts as makeshift clothes hangars. He made a mental note to buy some potent magnets the next time he was out.

Actually, thinking about it, lots of ideas came to him now. He could turn her into a real-life Pinhead like one of his favourite characters from the film, Hellraiser. He brought another nail and considered where to hammer it.

Am I a Monster?

Her eyeballs perhaps, as though performing a lobotomy. Through her tongue so he could hang his jacket there—the ultimate tongue piercing. He decided instead on banging it through the lips of her vagina, essentially stitching them together. The nail entered easily merging the walls of her vagina together. When she took a piss the nail would probably get rusty and cause infection too. This girl wasn't ever having kids. And if Rob wanted to fuck her, he'd have to find another hole.

"Call this triple punishment for not finishing your chores properly and for screaming for help before. Neighbour was about to call the police thanks to you. So, I'll give you ten minutes to recover a bit then you can finish your duties. Sounds fair?"

But Sarah was barely conscious, mumbling something unintelligible, occasionally a spasm rippling through her.

"Meh, fuck it," he said and went to grab a beer and watch TV.

An hour later with Sarah still sprawled on the sofa, there was a knock at the door. Andrew peered through the spy hole half expecting Eric to be there again but was pleasantly surprised to see Rob and his other friend, Kevin, standing there.

"Hey, what's happenin'. Come in!"

They did so and were slightly surprised to see Sarah on the sofa. It was the first time she'd been out of her room.

"I figured it was time she started earning her keep around here. But look at her, lasted ten minutes and gave up. Had to teach her a little lesson."

Rob and Kevin headed over to her and winced when they saw the nail heads protruding from her nipples. Then Kevin noticed something glistening by her vagina and winced again.

"Ooh, that's nasty, Andrew. She must have been a real bitch to have deserved that."

"She was screaming out the window yesterday, for help. Can you believe it? Neighbour fucking cornered me and started complaining. Was gonna phone the police and everything."

"What a bitch. Some people don't appreciate nothin'. Good job the neighbour never said nothin' or we'd all be in right trouble. But yeah, you put her to work, layin' about all day doin' fuck all. That's why we came over, actually. We was feeling a bit horny, like, but with her fuckin' pussy nailed shut, not a lot happenin' there, I guess."

"Yeah, sorry about that but I was pissed off and figured she had to learn a lesson. You'll have to find another hole to use, I suppose." Andrew shrugged, finished his beer and threw the empty can at Sarah.

Kevin and Rob looked at each other dubiously, then the bruised and emaciated body of Sarah, drool dribbling down her chin, snot dripping from her nose, blood seeping from the wounds to her nipples.

"You know what," said Rob. "I think I'll pass. Kinda puts me off looking at her now."

"We could fuck her mouth?" said Kevin. "Actually, yeah, you're right. Bitch. Not even worth a fuck anymore. So what is she good for?"

"Writing novels and that's about it," moaned Rob.

"Well, she still needs to learn about commitment and respect," said Andrew. "I say she learns the hard way. Lazy fucking slob."

Rob and Kevin grinned while simultaneously lighting up cigarettes. As an afterthought, Rob held the flame from his lighter against one of the nail heads, heating it up.

"Oh, that's nasty!" chuckled Kevin. "You think the

Am I a Monster?

whole nail is heating up, like inside her tit as well?"

"I guess we'll find out."

There soon came the smell of burning flesh. Around the nail the flesh started bubbling and sizzling. Sarah was suddenly woken from her semi-conscious stupor. She twitched and spasmed, clutching at her breast, trying to scream but seemed to be too weak to do so. Instead, she turned over onto her stomach.

"Nice one, Rob."

Kevin finished his cigarette and stubbed it out by pushing it up Sarah's butt. Rob did the same shortly afterwards.

"Well, I guess we ain't having no fun with her today. Better let her sleep it off, I s'ppose. We can come back tonight. Maybe another game of noughts and crosses," said Rob.

All three agreed and decided to go watch the local football team play nearby. It was a sunny day for once, after all. A shame to waste it. They left Sarah where she was but tied her hands behind her back and put duct over her mouth just in case. The last thing they wanted was Sarah trying to escape again.

Chapter 18

2 Months Later

Death. The only thing on Sarah's mind whether she was awake or asleep. When she was awake and begged Andrew or any of the others to just put her out of her misery they laughed in her face and beat her some more. Often with their hands or fists but usually with whatever was close by. Even an umbrella had been beaten over her head and then she was prodded so hard with it in the stomach, it bent. The mop and broom handles had also been broken over her head from repeated beatings which infuriated Andrew even more, blaming her for now having to go and buy new ones that he beat her even harder. Andrew had two dumbbells he used to build his muscles with and one of his favourite tricks was to kick Sarah to the floor and drop them on her. One time he missed and dropped it on her head instead. A lump the size of a golf ball had grown on the back of her head, which Andrew had taken great delight in popping with a hot sewing needle.

She thought there was a very good chance she had internal bleeding too. When she went to the toilet squeezing out a few drops of urine left her in excruciating agony, the urine mixed with blood. The nail still pierced to her didn't help either. The other two in her nipples had perhaps gone rusty because now her breasts were an odd colour, a purplish hue to them steadily growing out across the rest of her body, veins prominent. After Andrew, Rob was the most sadistic out of all of them. He used her as an ashtray, stubbing out his cigarettes on her body, face, neck, whatever was

Am I a Monster?

closest. Her body was thus also a mass of blisters and sores. He liked to torment her too, burning her with his cigarette lighter on her extremities. He even tried to set fire to her eyelids at one point, pinching them between his fingers, but Sarah had recoiled so violently and screamed so loudly, even Rob was alarmed.

She was allowed one sandwich, the bread mouldy and filled with whatever he found in the bin and one glass of warm water every two days, meaning she lost more than half her original weight and suffered constantly from dehydration. At least once a day she was subjected to some kind of torture, even by Karen who now acted distant from her, refusing to even look her in the eye. Sarah suspected Andrew had done something to her too for trying to help.

And when she was allowed or capable of sleep, assuming the agony her body was constantly suffering permitted such a thing, she dreamed of dying. No longer fantasies of writing best-sellers from her office in a mansion with a football star husband and cheerful kids running around, but of being surrounded by death. The plants wilted and dead, birds and animals like roadkill everywhere rotting away, the sky grey and grim, the seas and lakes all but dried up. She would find herself wandering along a desert landscape always on the verge of collapsing through hunger and starvation, her body reduced to a mere skeleton, looking for somewhere she could just curl up and die. But as though in some kind of purgatory, such a place was denied her and she was forced to walk and walk and walk, even though the skin and flesh on the soles of her feet had long since scraped away. She wanted to find death but even that had abandoned her to her miserable fate.

More often than not, though, such nightmares were short-lived. Andrew and the others found it amusing to wake her in the middle of the night, force her to listen to death metal music at full volume through headphones. The same song repeated again and again. They would force her to sniff amphetamine when she was on the verge of passing out, so she was denied such luxuries. Or they would make her dance for them, using various implements she would be told to insert inside her or further beatings would ensue. By now, she couldn't even remember her parents' names anymore, let alone any thoughts of her father rescuing her. She was alive but dead, a zombie, functioning on autopilot, made to clean up after the friends' parties. They purposefully made a mess when they went to the toilet. If Rob took a shit, he would make sure that some of it spurted onto the floor and the outside of the bowl and Sarah would be forced to scoop it up with her hands. Then, of course, she would vomit and then have to clean that up too. Or eat it.

Andrew made it perfectly clear to her that he wouldn't give her the satisfaction of dying; he would keep going until he either tired of her or died himself or was somehow captured. He told her how the police had virtually given up on finding her ever again, dead or alive, how Eric and especially her mother were broken wrecks, how her name had even been forgotten by the media. She was dead in everyone's eyes, except in his and his friends.

Sarah was so broken herself now, so weak, Andrew often went out for the day and didn't even bother tying her up anymore. She could barely walk, having to shuffle more often than not on knees and elbows to do the chores. Any idea of screaming out the window was abandoned after a second or two, her throat too painful to attempt such an elaborate manoeuvre. They were on the third floor of a block of flats anyway, with a busy street below, cars and buses and vans a constant. No one

Am I a Monster?

was going to hear her. She might as well whisper instead for all the good it did her.

Today was one such day she was left alone. Somehow, she had found the mental strength to figure a plan on how she might end this once and for all. Unable to walk, she crawled to the kitchen and managed to push herself up to the drawers where the cutlery was. Two of her fingers were broken in her right hand where Kevin had been curious and wanted to see how far back he could bend them before they snapped. So, with her left hand she rummaged in the drawer until she found a knife then slid down to the floor again. She tried to slice her wrists but her much weaker left hand couldn't harness enough strength for such a simple job as that. Not deep enough to do serious damage anyway, so she tried to slit her throat instead. Again, a waste of time. Sarah crumpled onto the cold, tiled floor and begged for death. Once more.

###

Eric left dejected the main entrance to Northgate Hospital for the Mentally Impaired, got into his car and held his head in his hands. He was sobbing but barely aware of it. Tina had finally succumbed to the mental anguish of her beloved daughter not being found, perhaps lying in a ditch somewhere being eaten by bugs, rodents and foxes, and this was what she couldn't get out of her head. It was that or she was being used as a sex slave somewhere, forced to make movies and would never be heard of again. Whatever her fate, it was a terrible one and no sedatives worked to allow Tina a moment's respite at night. Then, when she tried to commit suicide herself by taking an overdose of said sedatives, Eric and Tina's family had been left with no choice.

That had been a month ago, now two months had

passed and everyone it seemed had given up on everything. Sarah's disappearance wasn't even mentioned in the local newspapers anymore, much less on TV. The task force set up, despite Eric's insistence, had no choice but to dismantle and move to other cases. Ronald said he would continue to work on it in his own time, as he knew Eric would, but the Chief Inspector insisted the case was filed as unsolved. Tina lived in a perpetual state of depression and tears and was practically unresponsive to everyone, so Eric was on his own, spending the day sleeping whatever hours he could on the sofa. Tina's family had long since returned to their own home.

But he refused to give up the search.

He'd die himself before he gave up. That or until she came home. He followed Andrew as often as he could, sitting near his block of flats just waiting for something, anything he could use against him. When he followed Andrew around the streets, the kid acted as if Sarah had never existed, laughing and joking with a small group of friends who seemed to follow him everywhere. They played football together with other kids, played pool and darts in pubs despite being underage. It was May now and the weather was warmer, which meant he was out longer hours. In a week's time, school would finish, they would all take their exams and go their separate ways. Sarah should have been studying along with them, perhaps doing book signings as well. Even the publishers of her book had been forced to abandon the project for the time being, although they promised that if Sarah ever returned alive, it would be published.

Even Shelly, Sarah's best friend appeared to have accepted Sarah's fate and Eric no longer kept her informed of events because there were none to give. But Andrew, he was the key to all this. Eric knew with total

Am I a Monster?

certainty. He'd seen a girl with them occasionally, the one he recognised from the first time he went to the flat. He discovered her name was Karen Smith. He'd been unable to catch her alone and question her some more, but this was on his list. The trouble was that she was virtually inseparable from her boyfriend, who Eric knew as Dave. There were two other friends of Andrew; a kid he knew to be named Kevin and another Rob. Those two spent inordinate amounts of time in Andrew's flat and whenever they did leave—always together—they would do so as if they'd just had the time of their lives, laughing and joking, patting each other on the back, but Eric could never get close enough to find out what was the source of their entertainment.

But his famous hunch, his intuition, told him Andrew was involved with Sarah still somehow. The kid had also stopped joining the search parties which were now limited to once a month. He didn't know how he was going to do it but he needed to get back in that flat. In the meantime, also find a way to separate Karen from her boyfriend and the others. As long as his heart kept beating, he would find his daughter one way or the other. Even if it killed him in the process.

###

Karen lived in a state of permanent terror. She supposed she always knew it would happen but subconsciously she hoped Andrew would pretend he didn't know and would continue with his torture and persecution of Sarah as before. But, of course, Andrew was a control freak, needed to know everything that was happening around him and if someone went against him, it would only be a matter of time before he made them pay. And so he did.

She had been walking home after leaving Dave at his place and noticed someone was following her. Being dark and foggy, a quick glance behind her failed to reveal the person's identity and so she started walking faster. As did her pursuer. She was just about to break into a full-on sprint when Andrew called her name. The fact he had been following her for almost ten minutes without calling her should have been enough of a warning sign, but the shock and to a certain extent relief at hearing his name and not some stranger's had made her stop.

"Fuck's sake, Andrew, I thought it was some perv or weirdo following me. You scared the hell outta me!"

But Andrew wasn't smiling. Karen was within spitting distance of her home. She could see movement in the living room behind the curtains. Her mother probably pacing about as she always did when Karen was late coming home. She looked at Andrew's face and knew from the way he glared at her, that she was in trouble. She considered making a run for home, but he must have sensed it because he gripped her arm tight and dragged her into the shadows.

"Hey, Andrew, you're hurting me. What's wrong?"

"You're hurting me too, Karen. You really hurt my feelings, everything. I trusted you. All of you. We have a really good thing going but I guess there always has to be someone that fucks things up."

"What are you talking about?"

But she knew the answer already. Giving Sarah a tampon had been her mistake, and when she found out what he'd done about it, she had wanted to cry.

"You were in my flat, with your boyfriend, and my new flatmate, there to have whatever fun you wanted to have, and I was cool with that. That's why I gave Dave my spare key, for that precise reason, and also to keep an eye on her. I didn't give him the key so you could go there and try and...try and *help* her. Who the fuck gave

Am I a Monster?

you permission to do so? It sure as fuck wasn't me, so what gave you the right to take her food and help plug her leakages? That's going behind my back, Karen. That's betraying the trust I had in you. That's how you treat your friends, is it?"

"I...I was just...I'm sorry. I just thought like if I didn't she might bleed out on you and you wouldn't want that, so, I just gave her a spare one I had with me. It was jus—"

He slapped her across the face, hard. Then, he grabbed her arm and spun her around, pushing her arm up high behind her back.

"Ow! Andrew, you're gonna break it. It hurts. I'm sorry. I won't do it again."

"I know you won't do it again. Maybe I should give you something to think about just in case though."

He pressed his crotch against her, an erection already forming. "Maybe I should stick something in you just like you did to her. What do you think? That's fair, right? Or maybe I should drag you back home and set fire to your dirty little pussy, just like I did Sarah's."

With his free hand, he fumbled with the buttons on her jeans, eventually managing to unbutton them and pushing her trousers down. "That fair, Karen? Or maybe you should give me a blowjob, show me how much you're sorry."

"No, Andrew, stop. Please. I swear I won't do anything like that again."

He spun her around and gripped her tightly around the throat, choking her, while with his other hand he gripped her vagina. "There has to be control, Karen, you understand that, don't you? If one loses control, one loses everything. Even one's dignity, and we can't be having that. Now, I could drag you back to the flat and do to you what we did to Sarah last night. I bet I could even get Dave to join in, he's that scared of me. But I won't. Not this time, because we're still friend's, right? And friends look out for one another. So take this as a warning, Sarah is mine, but she's also yours and Dave's as long as you want. But I catch you trying to help her again, I will take you to the flat, rip off your clothes and stick a firework up your arse. Then ignite it, got it?"

She nodded in relief, yet not quite sure if he was bluffing or not. He liked playing mind games with people.

"Good, now fuck off. I'll see you at mine tomorrow night."

Karen pulled up her jeans, buttoned them up and ran without looking back. She didn't even tell Dave what had happened; instead, she sobbed herself to sleep wishing someone would stop Andrew somehow and lock him up for the rest of his shitty life.

As ordered the following evening she and Dave headed to Andrew's flat. Rob and Kevin were already there tormenting Sarah who was sat between them on the sofa. It was warmer now, but Karen never understood how Sarah didn't die from pneumonia in the cold winter months. She hadn't worn a single piece of clothing since she'd been kidnapped, showing every cigarette burn, scar, gash and bruise on her body. Her ribs threatened to poke through the thin walls of her chest, her cheekbones were like boulders, and she seemed to find it hard to hold her head high. It was as if she was constantly dozing off only to suddenly wake up again. And her breasts, which by now were almost non-existent, were a horrible greenish-yellow colour. Rob was tugging at the nails in her nipples, then setting light to them again. Sarah groaned and tried to flick his hand away as though swiping at a troublesome fly. Kevin kept stepping on her broken toes, using her ears as an ashtray, inadvertently

Am I a Monster?

touching them with the lighted end of his cigarette. Karen felt sick.

"Hey, happy couple!" said Rob, sweaty and smelly as always. Now that it was getting warmer, it would be like standing next to a blocked sewage pipe.

"What's happenin'?" asked Dave. Karen said nothing.

"Sarah here hasn't been doing the housework like she's supposed to," said Andrew. "So we decided it was time to teach her a lesson again. Your turn, Karen."

She knew it. She'd known since Andrew's threat last night that he would make her do something to Sarah, to show he was in control, knowing Karen never really wanted to get involved. Andrew had a plastic beer bottle in his hand. He finished the contents then handed it to Karen. Then he gave her his lighter.

"You know that water boarding thing they do to prisoners? Like the CIA and stuff. I thought of a better idea. Hold the bottle over her face, Karen."

Too terrified to argue with him, she did as she was told.

"Now set fire to the bottom."

Again, she did as she was told. The plastic bottle began to melt, dripping hot plastic onto Sarah's face while Rob and Kevin, both chuckling, held her thrashing body tight. It sizzled as it landed on her skin, burning into the flesh causing a sickening stench to fill the air. As Sarah somehow found the strength to scream, the plastic dripped into her mouth too, burning her gums, throat and lips.

"They used to do this in medieval times, you know," said Andrew, grinning. "They'd pour molten lead into the victim's mouth, effectively suffocating them. Not before sending them into extreme shock, of course. Amazing don't you think, Karen?"

She nodded, not wanting to look but knowing that if she showed any sign of regret, Andrew might punish her as well. Eventually, nothing remained of the bottle except the tip she was holding. The stench of burning flesh and plastic was overwhelming. In that moment, Karen decided that one way or another she was getting out of this.

Am I a Monster?

Chapter 19

Eric was sitting in his car with all the lights off between two vans to try and keep the bright police car as inconspicuous as possible. It was around eleven at night when he finally saw Karen and her boyfriend leave the block of flats. Dave had his arm around her and from the way she was waving her arms, and wiping her eyes, she seemed upset and agitated. Vulnerable. He couldn't hear what they were talking about but from their body language they were arguing over something. Eric climbed out of his car and made a discreet way towards them.

They were several metres ahead, but Karen was sobbing and saying something about having had enough, never again. That she wanted to run away as far as possible from Andrew. Dave was trying to get her to calm down and quieten down, but she was barely listening. Whatever had just happened in Andrew's flat had upset her a lot.

Eventually, they reached a crossroads and stopped. Eric darted into a shop entrance and hid, while Dave and Karen continued arguing a little longer then went their separate ways. Eric peeked out from his hiding spot, waited until Dave was gone then followed Karen. Already knowing where she lived, he followed at a good distance until she reached her street. Then he made his move.

"Hey, excuse me!"

She stopped. He saw her visibly tense, she didn't turn around, which he thought odd.

"Hey, Karen, right? I'm Eric, we met a while ago at Andrew's block."

Then she did turn around, but there was no look of relief on her face as if she'd been convinced she was being stopped by a dangerous individual. Quite the contrary, she looked nervous as she saw the police uniform, glancing behind her in the direction of her home.

"It is Karen, right?"

She nodded.

"Good. I don't know if you remember but I saw you coming out of the block of flats where Andrew lives last week. I'm Sarah Greenwood's father, the girl that went missing."

She nodded again, wiping her eyes. Even in the relative dark, the only light a streetlamp across the road, he could see her eyes were bloodshot and puffy.

"I remember. What do you want?"

"I just wanted to ask you a couple of questions. You just came from Andrew's flat, right. You seem pretty upset about something. Anything happen up there you want to talk about?"

She shook her head. "No. It was just...an argument, nothing else."

"An argument with Andrew?"

"No. Yes. Look, is this why you stopped me? I have to be home, my mother will worry."

"I understand. But this is important. I've been watching all of you for a while now. Especially Andrew. He's a good friend of yours, right? I imagine you all chat about everything. He seems pretty happy lately. Is he happy?"

"I guess so."

"Does he...do you chat about Sarah, my daughter very often? Does he still participate in the search parties?"

"I don't know, he doesn't really say. Look, I have to

Am I a Monster?

go, my mum will—"

"Yes, I know, Karen. I'll vouch for you if necessary. So, does he talk about Sarah very often?"

She flinched when he mentioned Sarah's name. Years of working as a police officer had given Eric an eagle eye when it came to determining the slightest reaction. The name Sarah made her uneasy.

"Sometimes he does."

"Did you know Sarah very well?"

She shrugged. "Just from seeing her around at school. Not very well. I have to go now so—"

"I think Andrew has something to do with her disappearance. Am I right, Karen? Does he know more than he's letting on? Because as someone whose girlfriend was kidnapped and hasn't been seen since, he doesn't act like a grieving boyfriend to me. You can tell me in complete confidence, you know. I just want to find her again, alive or dead, it doesn't matter now.

"Her mother had to be admitted to Northgate, you know. She was suicidal. And I think Andrew is somehow responsible. So you want to tell me what you know? Because what I know is that Sarah wasn't kidnapped by a stranger. It had to be someone she knew. Andrew."

Karen's features contorted into a look of anguish and despair. She started sobbing again, refusing to meet Eric's glare.

"You can tell me, Karen, I promise it's between you and me. Does he have her somewhere? In that flat? Is that why you and Dave were arguing just now? Why you were sobbing? You feel guilty about it. He made you all keep quiet, right? Tell me, Karen."

"Yes! It was Andrew that took her. He kidnapped her and did, does, horrible things to her. He makes us do things and I don't want to anymore. He cornered me here last night, told me that if I tried to help her or anything, he'd tie me down and do the same things to me as he did to her!

"And what they're doing is terrible. Me and Dave, we didn't want to do that. We thought he just kidnapped her as like punishment 'cause she pushed him the night before he took her and he got angry. When he gets angry, and loses control, he's a fucking psycho. Everyone's scared of him. And this has gone too far. I don't know how Sarah can still be alive—it's impossible!"

Eric was stunned. His legs threatened to give away, send him tumbling to the ground. He had always suspected Andrew might be involved somehow, being the last one to see her alive, but another part of him had also accepted the fact—albeit subconsciously, and he would never admit to anyone—that Sarah was dead. Buried somewhere, probably in someone's garden, never to be seen again unless someone stumbled upon her skeleton. But to hear that she wasn't dead, was still alive from what Karen was saying and that Andrew was indeed involved, shook him to the core. It took him several seconds to regain his composure, process everything he had just heard. Because something still didn't make sense.

"So, Karen, listen to me. She's still alive?"

"Yes. Barely, I guess, but yes."

"And he has her in his flat? The one you just came from?"

She nodded.

"But…I went there before because I always suspected he might be involved somehow so on the pretence of needing to use his toilet I went in and pretty much searched the whole flat, but she wasn't there."

"I know. He told us. He gagged her and tied her underneath the bed just before he let you in. He was laughing about it, mocking you. But she's there now. But

Am I a Monster?

please, don't tell him I told you. He'll kill me if he finds out. Even if he goes to prison for twenty years, he'll come looking for me. He mustn't know!"

Now she looked on the verge of a panic attack herself, sobbing loudly, utter terror in her eyes. Eric's mind was reeling. Andrew had been laughing behind his back all the time. Sarah had indeed been there as he suspected when he went to the flat. If only he'd checked under the bed…

"Tell me, Karen. Be honest. Is she…bad? You don't have to tell me what has been done to her, but…how bad is she?"

"Bad. He's been starving her since he took her. She must weigh less than half what she did before. And…him and especially Rob, they did bad things to her. I cry myself to sleep every night when I think about it. I tried to help her. Me and Dave, we went to the flat when Andrew was out all day and took her a hamburger and a Coke and she needed a tampon because…well, because, so I gave her one of mine, then Andrew found out I'd been helping so that's when he threatened me."

Eric had seen first-hand torture victims. It was still fresh in everyone's minds the terrible things the kids had been through over in Belton. He had sobbed himself for days afterwards through sheer relief. And now, here he was replaying it all once more. Something that should never have happened ever again.

Now, his mind was racing. His immediate desire was to rush to Andrew's flat, kick the door in if he had to and rescue his daughter, but he needed to think. Panicking wasn't going to help, but the desire was overwhelming. What if she died in the next few hours? According to Karen, she was in a bad way. Plus, he hadn't seen the other two kids leave. If Andrew was as sick and twisted as Karen was saying he would do whatever it took to save himself. Maybe even die in the process rather than go to prison, and three against one, strong as Eric was, was still too many without a weapon.

"Okay, thank you so much, Karen. I'll take care of it from now on. I won't say you were involved or anything. I'm going to go get a search warrant right now, so I suggest you go home, tell your boyfriend to keep away from the place. I'll be in touch."

"Okay, thank you. I'm so sorry about what happened but understand Andrew would have done the same to us. We were both so scared but make him pay for what he did. Make sure he spends the rest of his life in prison."

"Prison might be too good for this kid. We'll see."

And with that Eric hurried off to his car, searching for Ronald's number in his phone as he did so.

Am I a Monster?

Chapter 20

"One of the kids he hangs out with confessed everything, Ronald. Sarah is there right now. They've been torturing her. She may be barely alive, so we have to act right now."

Eric paced about Ronald's living room, unable to contain himself. He had insisted Ronald phone the judge right there and then, and if not to just go straight to Andrew's flat and kick the door down if necessary, but Ronald had told him to slow down and wait, repeating everything Karen had said. He did so as quick as possible making sure not to mention Karen's name.

"But wait, you said you went to the flat—even though I specifically told you to stay out of the case—but she wasn't there? You didn't see her or any signs she had even been there?"

"No. I told you. The kid's friend told me it was because Andrew had her gagged and bound under the bed. I was just about to check when Andrew caught me snooping."

"But I don't get it. If it had been my daughter, I would have looked anyway. What's he going to do? Beat you up?"

"Yes, I know, but, like you said, I didn't see anything in the flat that looked suspicious. Well, in that room it smelled funny, even though there was a window wide open. And there were suspicious looking stains on the bed and the carpet. They looked like blood but I couldn't be sure, so I pretended I'd gone in the wrong room and left.

"This girl, she says, Andrew has been starving her. She's been kept naked since she was kidnapped so

Andrew probably threw away or burned her clothes. You need to get that search warrant, Ronald. Right now."

"Hang on, hang on. So you saw what you thought to be blood stains, a weird smell even though the window was wide open, yet Andrew caught you about to look under the bed which is where your daughter was supposedly bound and gagged, and he did nothing? Acted as if nothing was wrong?"

"Yes, because he's a psycho, able to control his emotions like any serial killer. Listen, are you going to get that warrant or what?"

"Eric, I understand your desperation, I really do, so I'll overlook the way you're talking to me in my own home in the middle of the night but listen to yourself. You're asking me to wake the judge, and demand a search warrant based on something one of his so-called friends told you? A friend, I might add, who is so distraught about what they've all been doing to your daughter, she had to wait nearly three months to tell you?"

"Yes, I know, because she was scared for her own life and—"

"Look, Eric, this is what I'll do. I'm not phoning the judge yet until I have more reason to ask for a warrant, but I'll have a detective bring Andrew in for questioning. Right now, if you like. Then, according to what he says, we decide our next move. I'll even question him myself."

"But, if you're going to go to his flat and bring him in, you could check the flat while you're there. Wouldn't take five minutes and then you'll know."

"Well, we'll ask him if he will let us look around but if he says no, there's nothing we can do."

"But this is insane! My daughter could be dying as we speak!"

Am I a Monster?

"Then let's get a move on. I can't have you present during the interrogation, but you can wait outside if you want."

"Fuck, Ronald. If she is in there and something happens, I'll...I'll..."

But Ronald was already on the phone to one of the detectives.

An hour later, Eric watched as Andrew was brought in. He failed to notice Eric in the far corner, discreetly watching, but he looked perfectly calm, as if this was all some big mistake. He had refused to let them into his flat though, as Eric had expected. After another fifteen minutes, Ronald came out of the interrogation room to find a nervous, angry Eric pacing up and down.

"He's denying everything, Eric. Says he has nothing to do with Sarah's disappearance. Hasn't even asked for a lawyer to be present. By law, an adult must accompany him anyway, but he says his mother will probably be drunk and won't answer the door but he didn't mind either way. Is just happy to help clear up the confusion. His words, not mine."

"So why wouldn't he let your men in his flat to search it?"

"Said he had company and didn't want to embarrass them."

"Bullshit."

Ronald shrugged his shoulders. *I know but whadaya do?*

"Okay, keep pushing him. Tell him you have a witness or something, I dunno. I'm going home anyway; I need something stronger than coffee right now. Keep me informed, okay, for good or bad. I doubt I'll sleep but I'll only be on the sofa as usual."

"Now that's a good idea. You look like you could do with some rest, and I promise I'll let you know how it goes. Now, get outta here."

Eric did but he had no intentions of going home to bed. He couldn't even if he wanted to—his nerves wouldn't let him. Instead, he got in his car and drove to Andrew's block. There was no way he could sit there waiting for Andrew to be inevitably set free while his daughter could be up there. Despite Ronald's dubiousness, Eric believed Karen completely. He'd seen the terror in her eyes, Ronald hadn't.

He arrived and parked directly outside—no need to hide anymore with what he intended on doing. He checked to make sure he had two sets of handcuffs with him, although he wasn't sure if he would be using them and headed to Andrew's flat. This was it, the culmination of three month's searching. If Karen was lying and Sarah wasn't in there, alive or dead, he thought he might go crazy with grief right there and then.

His heart a manic thing in his chest, he took a deep breath and knocked on the door, his back to it so they wouldn't recognise him through the spy hole. Assuming anyone other than Sarah was in there, of course, because this Rob and Kevin might have gone home. But after a few seconds when he was about to kick the door in anyway, he heard footsteps and muffled whispering. When he heard a lock being unlatched and the door handle turn, before the door even opened, Eric burst in.

A large, obese kid stood there, blocking his path. Even so, Eric pushed him out of the way and surveyed the situation as quick as possible. Another kid was sitting on the sofa, who he assumed to be Kevin, the smaller of the two. The living room stank of marijuana, a thick cloud in the room which almost made it impossible to determine the scene clearly, but it wasn't thick enough that he didn't see another person sprawled on the sofa. Someone Eric didn't recognise, and who at first glance

Am I a Monster?

thought was dead, a cadaver exhumed from a grave because the person looked like a zombie or one who has been in a terrible accident, mutilated beyond recognition.

Finally, Eric had found his daughter.

Chapter 21

He had to blink several times. It was as if time had stopped and he was frozen in place, his eyes deceiving him. Maybe it was a mannequin, a sex doll someone had punched a hole in and the air was slowly escaping. Something, anything, other than what he wanted to believe because it seemed impossible there was a naked human being there, much less a sixteen-year-old girl, the last time he had seen her with curly, gleaming black hair, unblemished skin and the whole world at her feet. This thing before him was a monstrosity, fake, a creature from some horror movie the kids had stolen off a movie set. There was no way that thing before him could be alive, let alone human. It reminded him of bomb victims or serious car crash casualties. But when the person or whatever it was turned its head slightly to face him, reached out a trembling, skeletal arm and gave the weakest of smiles, he knew it was true.

This impossibly living creature was his daughter. Not a single area of her body was free from gashes or bruises or cuts. The toes on her feet were bent in all the wrong ways and black as if she'd been walking through wet mud. Great clumps of her hair were missing, sores in their place, blisters everywhere, cigarette burns. Her breasts, which he remembered Sarah laughing in private about with her mother as they grew and him slinking away in embarrassment, were a rusty colour, swollen in all the wrong ways, veins snaking across them. But what shocked him the most was how skeletal she had become. Like long-term prisoners of war, her bones protruded from her body, ribcage prominent, face gaunt. He recalled in that moment his mother who had slowly

Am I a Monster?

wasted away as she died from cancer. Sarah presented the same aspect, her eyes haunted and dying, the sparkle in them perhaps lost forever.

But it was the horror of seeing with his own eyes what they had done to her that caused him to forget he was not alone. He crashed to the floor when the greatest bolt of agony he had ever known ripped through him, its epicentre his skull. The cloud of smoke in the room seemed to thicken even more. Everything became distorted, as though he was immersed in a great cloud or was lying underwater. He couldn't even see his daughter now, she appeared to have vanished and Kevin was more like a ghost than human being as his image distorted and faded. He thought he heard voices but these seemed to come from a great distance and he couldn't understand what was being said. As though the lightbulb was flickering the light in the room grew darker then returned to its original brightness, like a strobe light in a nightclub. Eric tried to push himself up, aware something was very wrong, but his brain failing to make the connections as to what and he slumped back again, face pressed into the carpet.

Something heavy collided with his stomach and he was kicked onto his back. A ghost, or some terrible monster, was peering down at him, a lurid grin on its face, and it was only then did he have the faintest idea of what had happened. It wasn't a monster, but Rob, jeering and laughing at him. He pulled his foot back to kick Eric again, but now, he was starting to regain some of his senses. Rob must have hit him with something over the head, causing him to crumple to the floor, then kicked him. But as Rob's foot connected with Eric's stomach, the man grabbed it with both hands and gave a sharp twist with everything he had.

It worked. Rob was evidently not the quickest to react

to certain situations, probably given his size, because he flapped his arms in the air and crashed to the floor, that shook as he landed. His vision started to return now, so Eric pushed himself to his feet just as Kevin came running at him. This kid was no match for a fit, grown adult like Eric who deftly punched him on the nose that caused the kid's legs to buckle beneath him and he too fell. But Rob would be more of an issue. Eric turned to see him already pulling himself up. But the shock at seeing what they'd done to Sarah, remembering how Karen had said Rob was just as sadistic as Andrew, meant that the fury coursing through Eric's body would be too much even for this gigantic kid. When on his hands and knees, ready to leap at Eric again, Eric pulled back his right leg and kicked Rob as hard as he possibly could in the face. The last time he had done such a thing had been playing rugby at school and punting the ball up the other end of the pitch. It was perhaps just as well for Rob that his head was attached good enough to his neck or his head might have done the same as that rugby ball. His head whipped back sharply, the kid's nose exploding in crimson and he lay immobile and spread eagled on the carpet.

That kick contained everything that had been welling up inside Eric these last three months. He wished it had been Andrew's head but imagined his turn would come too at some point. For now, he turned his attention to Sarah. She was barely aware of what was going on as he squatted beside her, wanting to hug her but afraid to touch her at the same time, for fear of breaking her. Instead, he ran a hand across her brow, brushing a strand of hair from a swollen, bloodshot eye.

"It's going to be okay, baby. I found you. You're safe at last. I don't know what those bastards did to you, but they'll pay, okay. I promise. For everything. Can you

Am I a Monster?

move? Can you hear me?"

She muttered something unintelligible and shook her head feebly.

"It's okay, don't say anything. I'm gonna get you outta here, all right, and to a hospital."

Behind him, he heard movement. Kevin was pulling himself to his feet, groaning and clutching his nose.

"Unless you want me to break something else, you stay where the fuck you are, you got it?"

Kevin said nothing, but his eyes deceived him—he was looking for a weapon. A scenario where he was in prison and the same things being done to him as he had done to Sarah had no doubt replayed in his head and he didn't like the idea of that at all. Eric guessed he'd rather go down fighting than go through that. Which was fine with Eric. He stood up, ready to charge Kevin again when there was a noise none of them had expected.

The door opened and Andrew walked in.

Chapter 22

The look on Andrew's face was similar to that of Rob and Kevin when Eric barged his way in. A momentary look of shock and confusion, but this time, Andrew wasn't so slow to react. He quickly took in Rob sprawled on the floor, now regaining consciousness, Kevin with a broken nose and Eric poised ready to charge Kevin again, his arm pulled back, fist ready to go.

Andrew wasted no time. He ran at Eric and kicked him between the legs. It would have been a perfectly weighted kick had Eric not had the sense to turn at the same time, so Andrew's foot only caught him slightly in the balls, connecting mostly with his thigh. But it was enough to give him time. He threw a punch at Eric, smashing him in the cheek. Eric staggered back, his face cut into a sneer, eyes burning with rage, but so were Andrew's. He hadn't just spent two hours being interrogated after having been tricked and snitched by someone leading to this scenario. He had a pretty good idea who had told Sarah's dad the girl was here too—he'd deal with her as well once he finished with this.

There was no way he was going to juvenile then prison for what he'd done, so one way or the other it was going to end right now. Sarah was making some kind of a feeble attempt to get up, maybe to help her father, but she was in no position to help herself, falling back again onto the sofa. She was the last thing he needed to worry about now, anyway.

"You two, get the fuck up and stop him!" yelled Andrew.

Andrew had been doing a lot of muscle building with his dumbbells the last few weeks and had developed

Am I a Monster?

quite a muscular frame but even so, he still didn't think he'd be a match for Eric one on one. Not with the rage emanating from him right here in front of his daughter he'd been seeking for so long. Eric would kill him if he gave him the chance.

As if to prove the point, Eric turned to face him, spit and drool coming out of his mouth as he exhaled like some carnivorous creature. His hands were curled into fists, eyes burning.

"You are gonna pay for this, kid. For what you put us through, my daughter. You're a fucking monster. Even Northgate is too good for the likes of you. Look at what you've done to her! How could you? Another human being? A young girl?"

"She asked for it, Eric. I know that probably sounds unrealistic but it's true. She pushed me and not just physically. She made me out to look like a wimp, a coward, and that was never going to happen ever again. Not after all the other times. She was the one who paid—is paying—the price.

"And now, so will you."

Eric lunged for him, trying to grab him around the throat. He did so too, surprisingly fast, not giving Andrew time to react. He gripped Andrew's head with both arms and squeezed, blocking his wind passage, causing Andrew to choke and splutter. He waved at his friends who were still recovering from their blows. Andrew punched Eric in the ribs, the kidneys, but it was like punching a wall—the man barely flinched. Andrew could feel his chest tightening, his cheeks puffing out. He flapped his arms again at his two friends to help but they seemed uncertain. Were they going to betray him too like that bitch Karen did?

He rained blow after blow into Eric's side but seeing as it had no effect on him—quit the contrary, the man was squeezing his neck even harder—he did the only thing he could think of. He grabbed Eric's balls and squeezed as hard as he could. That did it. Eric groaned, tried to twist to his left, out of reach of Andrew's hand but it was impossible. Andrew wasn't letting go until his own body gave up the fight.

The slightest release on Andrew's neck gave him his opportunity. He let go of Eric's balls, twisted himself and delivered an uppercut to Eric's chin. The man staggered back but he wasn't done yet. While Andrew coughed, getting the air back into his legs, Eric stepped back and toe-punted Andrew in the balls himself. He collapsed to the floor clutching his groin.

"You little piece of shit. Think you're tougher than me? I should kill you right now or maybe that would be too easy. Maybe I should do to you what you did to my daughter. All three of you."

He glared at Kevin and Rob who looked confused, watching the two battle it out. Eric wondered if they were trying to decide whether to run or help their friend. If Eric managed to subdue Andrew, they were going to prison too. They must have known this because as Eric took out a set of handcuffs, Rob shook his head, sneered at Eric and charged him.

The kid was too big, too heavy for even Eric to deal with. Rob collided with him and both went flying, crashing against a far wall. Eric slumped to the floor but immediately tried to get up again, knowing he had to be quick or he was in trouble. But he wasn't quick enough. Seeing his friend had made a decision, Kevin ran over and kicked Eric in the face as hard as he could. For the second time, the room turned cloudy, spinning, and Eric fell into darkness.

When Eric opened his eyes again thirty minutes later, Andrew went and stood over him. He'd used Eric's own

Am I a Monster?

handcuffs to chain him to the radiator. Beforehand, he had been forced to have serious words with both Rob and Kevin, telling them that they had very nearly caused the demise of all three of them. If they thought they were going to act like Karen and betray him, they were very wrong. The two apologised for their delayed reaction, blaming it on having been almost knocked out by the father. Andrew didn't entirely believe them, but it would have to do for now. Andrew knew fear and doubt in another's eyes when he saw it.

It was imperative that control be maintained. Right now, it was borderline. Karen had gone behind his back yet again committing the cardinal sin of informing Eric where his daughter was and now these two he suspected had been on the verge of running off as well. Lessons had to be taught and Eric was going to help teach them. Andrew went and fetched a knife and cut away at Eric's clothing leaving him naked.

"You know what will happen if he leaves this place alive, don't you?" he asked Kevin and Rob.

Both looked sheepish, surely knowing they'd fucked up by not helping Andrew immediately.

"Yeah, I know," said Kevin. "Look, I'm sorry. He hit me hard, the fucker. Stunned me he did. So yeah, he gotta pay for that and I ain't going to juvenile or prison man, no way."

Rob shook his head.

"It's okay, it's not your fault. Someone brought him here, told him Sarah was here, so if he leaves, we're all going to prison. They'll fuck us up inside. So we're going to fuck him up and make sure none of this gets out. I just got back from being interrogated at the station, they let me go, so no cops know he's here. It's going to stay that way. Right, Mr Greenwood?"

With his knife, he sliced off the man's nipples then

inserted the tip of the blade and twisted it in the wounds. Eric woke up, his eyelids fluttering, face contorted into a grimace. When he finally focused and saw the situation he was in, his eyes opened wide.

"Hey there, Mr Greenwood. Feeling comfortable?"

All this time, Sarah was struggling to sit up, no doubt in her befuddled, dazed state thinking she could help her father. And Andrew had every intention of ensuring she did.

"They know I'm here. The detectives will be here any moment and it's over, Andrew, so you might as well let me go and get it over with. You're going to prison for the rest of your life. You all are."

"Somehow, I don't think so. You came here alone without telling anyone. Knew they weren't going to pin Sarah's disappearance onto me, didn't you, so you figured you'd go it alone. Well, no worries, Sarah's gonna come and show her appreciation."

Andrew gave the knife to Rob and went and dragged Sarah over. She resisted feebly, groaning, trying to say something to her father but none could understand what.

"Come on, Sarah. Your daddy came to see you. Don't you want to say hi? Not very welcoming of you, is it?"

"You leave her alone. You've done enough to her already. Why don't you accept it's over and give yourself up? I told my boss it was you, that I had proof. If they see I'm not at the station in a couple of hours to clock out, they'll know where to look."

"Then I guess we better be quick, eh, Mr Greenwood. And besides, you're lying. If they had proof, they'd be here already. I told you."

The blood was pouring down Eric's chest, but he seemed barely aware. Andrew forced Sarah to squat in front of him. He pushed her face against his so her dad could give her one last kiss before leaving. Sarah

Am I a Monster?

practically fell on top of him.

"Aww, ain't that cute! Father and daughter finally reunited after all this time."

"Sarah, if you can hear me, I promise this will all be over soon. Reinforcements are on their way and this piece of shit and his cronies will be going to prison. Just stay strong, hang in there. You'll be at a hospital in no time."

"Daddy, thank you for saving me. I love you."

Andrew smiled. He was genuinely touched. He took the knife off Rob and put it in Sarah's hands, curling her broken fingers around the handle. Then, guiding her hand, he lowered it until the blade was caressing Eric's balls. Then he nudged her arm so the blade sank in. Eric tried to squirm his way free, but it was too late, blood and other secretions began to run down his thigh and collect on the carpet. Barely aware even of what she had done, Andrew raised her arm, directed the knife at Eric's throat and pushed her. The blade sank into Eric's neck up to the hilt, blood spraying everywhere from a severed jugular and covering Sarah's face and body. Eric gurgled and choked, eyes wide in shock but never leaving his daughter's crimson face. Several seconds later, he stopped gurgling and keeled over, dead.

"There you go. Good job, Sarah. Well done! He was only going to interfere anyway. As a treat, I think I'll buy you a hamburger. How does that sound?"

Sarah could only shiver and tremble, tears running down her wet face coursing lines in the blood now splattered everywhere. Andrew meanwhile grabbed his phone and dialled Karen, telling her both she and Dave needed to come urgently. There were important developments.

Chapter 23

While they waited for Dave and Karen to appear the three boys dragged Eric's body to the spare bedroom and left him there still bleeding out on the carpet. It was going to take a lot to get these stains out of the carpet, if it was even possible. Andrew wasn't sure, he'd never tried before, and as much as he forced Sarah to comply with her chores, he didn't think she was in much condition for hard scrubbing either. A shame. Maybe he'd have to buy a rug instead to cover them.

They returned to find Sarah still weeping on the floor where Eric had been handcuffed. Andrew removed those as well and put them in his pocket. While he knew Eric had been lying about the other detectives knowing his whereabouts, he hadn't been lying about the fact that when Eric failed to return to the station, their immediate suspicions would fall on him. It was too coincidental, after he'd only a few hours earlier been interrogated at the station. And then it occurred to him Eric's police car was probably parked somewhere close by. None of them knew how to drive—that was a problem. But if everything worked out as planned Eric's body would be disposed of relatively quickly.

"What are we gonna do with the body, Andrew?" asked Rob as though reading his thoughts.

"Once Karen and Dave get here, they'll help us get rid of it. Between everyone, I figured we could dismember him then put his parts in rubbish bags and dump them somewhere. Should be easy, right?"

Kevin and Rob looked at each other dubiously and said nothing. They were probably counting how many years they might get in prison. Even though they weren't

Am I a Monster?

responsible for his death, as accessories to murder—a police officer, to boot—no jury or judge would be lenient with them. Especially as he was the father of the girl that had gone missing too. Andrew knew in that moment that if detectives did discover the truth he would kill himself rather than face the wrath of a horrified, angry public.

"You think Sarah is aware what she did?" asked Kevin as he stared at the girl slumped on the floor. "She just killed her own father. Stabbed him in the balls. How fucked up is that!"

"Oh, she knows," said Andrew. "I don't think she's in much of a state to care right now, though. Poor kid. She'll get over it."

If she wasn't careful, she was going to sprawl in the thick pool of her father's blood. Andrew picked her up and sat her down on the sofa, then dragged a table over to the radiator to cover the stain. There came a noise outside which caused all three to jump. Andrew hurried to the door and peered through the spy hole. He smiled and opened the door. Dave and Karen stepped in, looking nervous, keeping close to the door as though they might want to suddenly bolt.

"Hey! How it's going?"

"What the fuck happened?" asked Dave when he saw the amount of blood on Sarah's face and on the wall.

"Oh. That. Yeah, we had a, umm, visitor. An unwelcome one."

Karen was pallid, refusing to look Andrew in the eyes. She looked like she might throw up at any moment.

"Who? Who came? A neighbour?" asked Dave.

"Sort of. You got any idea who it was, Karen?"

She shrugged and shook her head.

"No? Well, that's weird. I wonder how he knew to come?" said Andrew more to himself than anyone else.

"Who, Andrew? Who the fuck did this?" asked Dave.

Evidently, Karen hadn't had time to tell him yet what she'd done. Maybe she was too scared. As she should be.

"Well, I got picked up and taken to the station for questioning about Sarah. Apparently, they received a tip-off saying that Sarah was here. I refused to let them in but went with them, and when I get back, who do you think I found in my flat, trying to rescue his daughter?"

"Her *dad*? Who the fuck knows she's here other than us?"

"No one, Dave. That's precisely my point. No one except those of us here right now. Which means one of you told him and I think we know who, don't we, Karen?"

Dave turned, incredulous, to his girlfriend, who looked up sharply and shook her head.

"Karen? You told the police Sarah's here? What the fuck were you thinking? We'll all go to prison!"

"It wasn't me! I didn't tell them anything! Eric already knew where Andrew lived, remember. He must...he must have followed you here and guessed you had Sarah here. I swear I didn't say a thing!"

"I don't think so, Karen. According to Kevin and Rob, when they opened the door, he barged in, knowing full well she was here. He used me as a decoy to get into the flat while I was being questioned. Because you told him. I can see it in your face, Karen. You look like you might throw up any second. And you look guilty as fuck."

She started sobbing. "I was scared, that's all! I thought you were gonna kill her then we'd all go to prison for life. I just wanted it to end. It's sick what's going on. You said you were just going to teach her a lesson and that's it. We'll, look at her, she looks like a fucking zombie!"

"I am teaching her a lesson. I didn't say when the

Am I a Monster?

lesson would be over though, did I?"

Karen tried to open the door and bolt, but Kevin and Rob had been expecting such a thing, so quickly pushed her away.

"Hey, leave her alone!" said Dave, but there was a quiver in his voice. He knew he was outnumbered and that if he tried to run with his girlfriend, they had no chance.

"Look, let's just calm down, right? You got her dad, no one else knows Sarah's here, so we're still okay. Karen's just scared, and yeah, man, I mean, I didn't expect it to go this far either. So let's just get rid of the body before anyone comes looking for him and have a few beers or something. I'll go get 'em. Like, lesson learned, right?"

"And the first thing you'll do is go running to the cops. Can't happen, Dave. She broke our trust. Our bond. If I hadn't got here when I did, we'd all be arrested right now. And when people fuck up, lose control of matters, everything goes to shit. Can't happen again. She's gotta pay for what she did. I can't trust her anymore."

"So…so what are you sayin'? Look, it was a mistake. She won't do it again, I'll make sure she don't."

Karen was huddled against Dave's shoulder, on the verge of screaming. Andrew wasn't sure, it was hard to tell from her dark jeans, but he thought she might have pissed herself. She made another desperate run for the door, but Rob was blocking her path. He threw her at Andrew.

"All I ever wanted was to have some real friends. People I could trust. Who would do what I said without questioning it. My dad taught me that one. If people do as you tell 'em, no matter what, they'll stay with you forever. I thought we had that here. I let you all fuck Sarah, do what you wanted with her, but someone had to fuck it up for everyone."

He gripped Karen tightly around the throat and threw her to the floor beside an immobile Sarah. "Looks like you got a busy schedule, Sarah. You can't do your fucking chores around this place, so you have to earn your keep in other ways. You already took care of your dad, now you can do the same to your new friend."

The knife he'd used on Eric, he put in Sarah's hand. "Cut her clothes off."

Sarah dropped the knife and shook her head. She seemed to be regaining something of her old self. Perhaps being made to kill her father had woken something in her, previously lost forever. Andrew sighed.

"See what I mean? When I lived with my parents, if I didn't do what I was told, without question, you know what they used to do? Kick the shit outta me. My dad used to put my head down the toilet and flush the chain. Sometimes after he'd just had a piss. Or worse. My mum would pull my trousers down, grab a pair of scissors and threaten to cut my dick off. Sometimes, she'd make little cuts in my balls, just enough for it to bleed a bit.

"That's what I went through when I refused to do something. When I was twelve, they were both pissed and off their heads on coke or something. My mum was on her period. They thought it would be funny for her to sit on my face and make me lick her pussy, all that blood dripping into my mouth. And you know what? I did it. Never even puked.

"So, when I say people gotta do as they're told, that's what I mean. Now, Sarah, pick up the fucking knife and cut your friend's top off."

Sarah must have heard him because she did as she was told—her hand trembling so much she almost cut herself in the process.

Am I a Monster?

"Good girl. Remember, you do as I say, I'll get you a Big Mac afterwards, like I promised. See, that's another thing I learned. Sometimes, you gotta treat people like kids or pets. They do as they're told, sometimes they get rewarded. Action equals reaction. Slice her top off."

Karen screamed and tried to push Sarah off, but Rob gripped both her arms and held them tightly behind her back. He was grinning, which made Andrew smile. Rob knew the score. Dave, meanwhile, seemed unsure of himself, whether to try and help Karen and risk being hurt himself or go along with it. Karen was pleading with him to do something, for Andrew to stop, but neither was listening. Dave looked like he might burst out crying any second. Having to use both hands, Sarah sliced through Karen's t-shirt, exposing her bra.

"That as well."

She did as she was told.

"Cut her tits off."

Karen screamed. She howled and spat and writhed on the floor, so much that even Rob struggled to contain her.

"Andrew, no!" said Dave, and made to go to his girlfriend. Kevin and Andrew kept him at bay.

"Do it, Sarah. Think of that juicy Big Mac. And remember, it was this bitch that brought your dad here in the first place. If she hadn't he would still be alive."

Sarah looked up into Karen's eyes. She was crying too in her zombie-like state. "I don't have a choice, I'm sorry."

She gripped one of Karen's breasts in her hand and began to slice. After a few seconds a fleshy lump came loose. Sarah dropped it then sliced off the other. Karen was too weak to scream any more by now. Her head rocked back and forth as though on the verge of falling unconscious.

"Good girl, Sarah. See, you know what I mean.

Obedience, that's what it all comes down to. Now, cut open her throat."

To Dave's howls of anguish, Sarah did. For the second time that night a gush of warm blood covered her face and body, some of it going down her throat. Once Karen was dead, Kevin and Andrew let Dave go who sank to the floor, sobbing loudly.

"No time to rest yet, Dave. Take your girlfriend to the bathtub and start dismembering her. If you don't, I'll dismember you. Alive."

It took a few warnings and threats and kicks but eventually Dave did so. Two hours later his girlfriend lay in several pieces in the bloody bathtub. Eric joined his ex-girlfriend an hour later. As promised, Andrew sent Kevin off to a nearby MacDonald's to grab burgers for everyone. Andrew thought they deserved it.

Chapter 24

Her memories were vague and distorted. Like her vision. Her body felt separate from the rest of her as though cut in two. Only the occasional stabbing sensation between her legs or the constant throbbing in her chest reminded her she was still intact. Sarah often felt as though she was floating, swimming in a dark, dense cloud. Light, she was so light she felt like she could float off if she so desired. And often she did. Occasionally, terrible memories and visions filled her mind, things so horrific they had to be hallucinations. Maybe memories of some horror film she'd seen recently. Her parents would be upset to know she watched such things, but she couldn't think where else they may have come from.

The hallucinations were extremely vivid too because when she looked down at herself and her vision managed to focus enough for her to take in what she was seeing, it was terrible. Her body was cadaveric, something someone had dug up from a grave and attached to her. So many burns and sores and scars. Her breasts felt the heaviest of all and when she dared to touch them, white hot bolts of agony shot up her chest. When this occurred, her throat felt as though it was on fire too. As if she'd hadn't drunk anything for weeks but she was too weak to go in search of water.

And one of the most terrifying hallucinations she had last night was seeing her father here, wherever here was. She couldn't remember the last time she'd seen him, maybe he was really busy at work or something or hadn't mum and dad said something about going to Barcelona on holiday? Maybe that was it; they'd gone for a much-deserved break and left her behind. That was okay. Dad worked such long hours and it must be terribly stressful. She was old enough to look after herself now so everything was fine.

Except it wasn't. If she was suffering vivid hallucinations and her throat and breasts and groin hurt so much it meant something was very wrong. There had been a group of boys here last night and a girl. Her dad had been present earlier then something happened and he had gone without saying goodbye. After that the girl had come with another boy and something bad happened and she had gone too. It was infuriating because it seemed so real—she thought she could still smell her father's aftershave in the room. Old Spice, the one he'd been using for years and which no one else seemed to use any more.

Sarah struggled to remember more. There had been shouting and screaming then laughter and she'd been left alone for a while. After that, one of the boys had gone out and come back with something that smelled so utterly fantastic she had been drooling. A hamburger, yeah that was it. MacDonald's. She remembered now. Her new boyfriend, Andrew, had handed her a Big Mac with fries and a Coca Cola and she had wanted to scoff that thing down so fast but Andrew had made her eat slowly so she didn't throw it all back up. It was as if she hadn't eaten something so wonderful in all her life. In fact, it was as if she hadn't eaten at *all* in her entire life. She could still taste it now, smell it even, and she thought she had burst out crying because she never wanted something so badly. Last night's dream had to be the most vivid and powerful one she had ever had.

She tried to sit up. If it had been a dream, it had been magical because it was as if eating that burger had restored much depleted energy levels in her body. It

Am I a Monster?

seemed that the last few weeks she had been too tired and too ill to do anything but sleep. Now though, she could feel her heart beating, albeit slowly, wiggle her fingers and toes although when she did that to her toes, sharp bolts of pain ran up her legs much like when she touched her breasts. Sarah recalled that happening before and the pain had sent her straight back to sleep again but now it had the opposite effect. Her eyes opened wider, the room wasn't so murky and cloudy anymore and she could almost make out objects around her instead of it all being shadowy like ghosts. When she pushed herself up further, her whole body groaned from a thousand different places, stinging and gnawing pains attacking her without mercy. Her head was going to explode through lack of liquids. Her tongue was stuck to the roof of her mouth and when she managed to wiggle it about she was shocked to find several gaps in her teeth.

Sarah raised a hand and wiped her eyes. It stung to do so but she really needed to know what was going on here. She was starting to get scared. She thought of calling out for Andrew but some primeval part of her told her this might not be a good idea. Why, she couldn't fathom. The lack of noise in the house suggested she was alone anyway. Finally, the blurriness cleared and she could see again, as if she'd been in a coma for weeks and her eyes needed adjusting. But when she looked down at herself she had to wipe them again because her earlier thoughts about her body being separate from her appeared to be true.

That wasn't her body, it couldn't be. It looked exactly like the one from her nightmare, only this time with the added touch of being covered in dried blood, smeared everywhere. Her breasts were a horrible purplish colour with thick veins snaking everywhere and were they pins or something where her nipples should be? The shock of what she was seeing caused adrenaline to snake through her veins giving her even more energy and strength to see clearer. Her emaciated body which looked as though it hadn't been fed in weeks was covered in bruises and cuts. Her vagina throbbed and when she looked, the crudest of piercings appeared to have been carried out on her but nothing like she'd ever seen before and evidently it hadn't been done cleanly because the area around it was swollen and bruised too. A murky liquid seeped constantly from her vagina and when she gently touched the area, her body shook with pain.

"What the fuck is this?" she muttered.

And her feet, that was why her toes hurt so badly. They were bent in all the wrong ways and the flesh and skin around them was also swollen and now a dark green colour. She didn't dare touch those but it was obvious they were broken. Had she been in a car crash or something? If so, for how long and why wasn't she in hospital?

Fragments of the past few days began to surface like sunken memories. She glanced around the room, at the floor and walls. They were covered in blood too as if a massacre had taken place here. Or maybe it was her blood after she'd been rescued from this car accident or whatever it had been. But a part of her knew she hadn't been in no accident. She sure as hell knew she hadn't consented to have her nipples and vagina pierced in such a crude manner and they were fucking cigarette burns on her body not burn marks from a car catching fire.

Then she saw the empty Big Mac boxes on the table, empty Coca Cola cups beside them. She stared at them as though they were ancient relics worth millions. She could still taste the ketchup at the back of her throat, which she'd thought odd. It meant that it hadn't been a dream then. Which also meant…

Am I a Monster?

Then she saw it. Laying by the radiator, underneath a table and a large stain which looked suspiciously like blood, was a watch, the metal strap broken. She knew that watch anywhere because she had bought it as a fortieth birthday present for her dad. The phrase '*Love you always*' was etched onto the back. Grimacing and wincing she eased herself off the sofa and crawled over to the table and picked up the watch. When she turned it over and saw the engraving, she dropped the watch as though it was a poisonous object. She slumped against the wall and replayed her most recent memories.

Specifically, where her father visited her last night. She had dreamt of eating a Big Mac and there was the empty box. She dreamt her father came to rescue her and then something happened to him she couldn't quite see, as if whatever it was had been so horrific her mind blocked it forever. Something involving a knife, her father naked for some reason, telling her he loved her. And then there had been blood, so much blood. Blood on her, the walls, the carpet, the watch. And the kids had been here, three of them. They had dragged him off then the other boy and the girl had come. The girl used to be her friend. She once brought her a burger as well. But then this girl had been covered in blood too and somehow Sarah had gotten it all over herself. A knife. A hunting knife. It had gone straight through her throat up to the handle. And it had been Sarah's hand that guided it.

As it had also been the one that sliced her father's throat open.

It was like a series of slides shown one at a time first then in one fast reel. Everything came flooding back. Her dad barging into the room, fighting with the two boys then Andrew coming in, what they forced her to do then to the girl as well. Then they had dragged the bodies to the bathtub and began the process of dismembering both while the other boy went to MacDonald's.

As a stunned Sarah tried to make sense of what had happened, everything else returned to her memory banks. Starting with the night she had pushed Andrew over causing him to cut his hands to shreds. She held up her hands and stared at them as if seeing them for the first time. These hands had brutally stabbed her own father, the one looking for her. Andrew had taken great delight in showing Sarah the press conference when he'd first kidnapped her and then making her watch every report on the news that involved her—the search parties, the offer of a reward, her parents once more begging for information while Andrew stood in the background shedding crocodile tears.

Tears ran down her face now, causing the dried blood on her cheeks and chest—her father's and Karen's blood—to run also. She could not recall every single thing that had happened to her over the last three months or so but the mutilation and torture to her body was clear to see. And her father and Karen had paid the ultimate price for it. Sarah was too stunned and shocked to even scream for the death of her father. Only one thing ran through her head instead.

Revenge.

Revenge like that woman had got who had been buried alive a few years ago in her own garden in the same village. The one with the cactus plant. She'd found some enterprising ways of getting her own back on her enemies. Sarah thought she could do the same too.

Chapter 25

"So we'll do it in stages. We can't take all of it at once anyway—it won't all fit in the car. The old man's is the biggest problem so while me, Rob and Dave take one load you start filling other plastic bags," said Andrew.

Kevin nodded. "Gotcha."

"Cool. Let's go. Grab a sack each and I'll do the same. We're gonna bury 'em out near Fritton so we'll be a couple of hours, I guess. If anyone knocks on the door, don't answer it. Don't even look to see who it is. Just stay dead quiet. Like Karen and Eric over there!"

He laughed at his own joke. The others did the same. From her position on the sofa, pretending to be asleep, Sarah could see the hatred in Dave's eyes. He was being forced to bury his own girlfriend after having been forced to dismember her. He hadn't said a word since they'd returned from wherever they went; she assumed to find someone willing to drive them out to Fritton with a very suspicious cargo.

Andrew, Rob and Dave went to the bathroom and each came back carrying a large plastic bag. Her father's remains were in those bags. He was being dumped out in the woods as though he was nothing but trash. He didn't deserve that, no one did. Except these kids, perhaps. Definitely. She would like nothing more than to dismember them all, preferably while still alive. She would love that more than anything. But she had to be clever. She was still extremely weak and one Big Mac wasn't going to magically give her the strength to overpower them. Especially Rob and Andrew. But she'd figure it out. She'd come too far to give up now. Her father's words echoed in her head again, the same ones as when she had first been kidnapped: *You're not just going to lie here and give up. Wait to die. I taught you better than that. If you at least try it's better than giving up.* Well, if she had to die, if her time had come, she wasn't going to go alone. She'd make damn sure of that much at least.

The three boys left leaving her alone with Kevin, the weaker of the four she thought. He was also the quietest and from what she could remember he had never really done a great deal to her after they originally raped her. But it didn't matter; he was just as guilty as the rest of them. She watched with one eye half open as he headed to the bathroom to start bagging body parts. Andrew was so confident of himself, he'd left both bodies in the bathtub overnight, saying no one was going to come looking for them yet and besides, he needed to find a driver. Someone he could trust.

She could hear him groaning and muttering to himself as he filled the bags. Sarah took the opportunity to grab the knife that was sitting on top of the table, still covered in Karen's and her father's blood. She hid it beneath her and waited for Kevin. He didn't take long, returning after a few minutes carrying two large black sacks. He left them by the front door and wiped the sweat from his brow.

"I don't blame you, you know," she said, pretending to wake up.

Kevin turned with a start to face her. "What?"

"I know Andrew made you all do what you did. You're scared of him but it's okay, I understand. I don't even blame you. Poor Dave, having to watch his girlfriend die."

Kevin made as if to say something then stopped. "Yeah, well, I'm sorry, okay. None of us meant for it to go this far. I don't wanna go to prison, but

Am I a Monster?

Andrew...yeah, he's a psycho. Doesn't act like that at school but in private...some of the things he did to his mother. I was told he threw her down the stairs when she was drunk, broke both arms and three ribs, then told her to get up and make his dinner. Which she did."

"Wow, that's terrible. What a horrible kid. I'm not surprised everyone's scared of him."

"Well, yeah. But look, I'm sorry about your dad too. If only Andrew hadn't come back when he did, this might all be over by now. Maybe they'll get stopped taking the remains to Fritton and you'll be freed. If I have to go to prison, I deserve it. For not saying anything."

"Aww, thank you. Why don't you come and sit here with me, rest a bit? After the Big Mac I had last night, I feel much better. Maybe I can do something for you to help you relax. After all, wouldn't be the first time, would it!"

Kevin looked both stunned and surprised at the offer. As far as Sarah was aware he didn't have a girlfriend and she thought he might have lost his virginity the first time he raped her. He'd certainly enjoyed the experience, coming back for more quite regularly until Andrew started disfiguring her. Kevin thought about it for a few seconds then came and sat beside her.

She gave him her best smile under the circumstances, which wasn't easy. It had been so long since she smiled her jaw ached after just a few seconds. She placed a hand on his lap. Immediately, she saw the rising bulge in his trousers.

"Stand up and pull your trousers down."

Still somewhat surprised by this unexpected turn of events, Kevin did so. Sarah took him in her mouth, waiting, hoping he would close his eyes, to revel in the moment. He did.

Sarah slowly brought out the knife, gripped his cock

with one hand and with one deft move, castrated him. Kevin's eyes shot open. A look of utter shock and horror replaced that of ecstasy. He shook, looked down at himself and saw the blood spurting everywhere, covering Sarah. A few seconds later, he crumpled to the floor.

"H-help," he croaked, his hands trying to stop the haemorrhaging and failing dismally.

"Help? You want me to help you? After all the help you gave me, now you want me to help you. What would you like me to do? Stitch it back on for you? Get some duct tape and stick it on? Give me some ideas, because when it comes to help, I'm at a bit of a loss."

"Please. Call an ambulance. Help me."

"Umm, let's just evaluate things shall we. For one thing I don't have a phone. Your friend smashed it up, remember? Second, where were you when I needed help? Not even a glass of fucking water. I would have drunk your piss I was so desperate and dehydrated, and now you ask me for help?"

"Please, I'm begging you."

His face was deathly white now and he was shaking, a pool of blood rapidly forming beneath him. She held up his tiny cock and dangled it in front of his face as though offering a dog a treat.

"I've been begging for months, Kevin. Months. You stood there while I was forced to kill my own father. Yeah, I'll help you."

Kevin keeled over and lay with his hands between his legs, now shaking violently. She sat beside him and put his cock in his mouth.

"Swallow it," she demanded, covering his mouth with her hand. He tried to spit it out, but using all her strength, she kept her hand there and with the other squeezed his nostrils shut. After a few seconds he gave up and was

Am I a Monster?

forced to swallow it.

She didn't think it was that big for him to choke but that was what he started doing. Maybe it went down the wrong way, she wondered, as she watched him splutter. It gave a whole new meaning to the phrase 'deepthroat'. He tried to ram two fingers down his throat to bring it back out again but failed to reach it. She decided to help him a little. Sarah took the knife and sliced his throat open performing a makeshift tracheotomy. His dick popped out, slimy and covered in mucus. Not really wanting to, but deciding to do so anyway, she picked it back up with the tips of her fingers and put it back in his mouth. Guessing that the others might be back at any moment, she took the blade, scooped out Kevin's eyeballs and popped them into his mouth as well to shut him up. She left him dying in agony while she pulled herself to her feet and prepared herself for when the others returned. One down, three to go.

Chapter 26

It was around twenty minutes later she heard the front door open. This had given her enough time to hobble to the kitchen, find something to eat and drink to help regain her strength and energy and prepare for when they entered. Some Aspirin in the cupboard too which she greedily swallowed then almost puked back up. She knew she couldn't single-handedly take them on one at a time so had thought of an enterprising way to perhaps take them on as a collective. If it didn't work, at least they were going to suffer as much as she did.

Once her plan was ready she had then tried to drag Kevin out of the way so he wasn't the first thing they saw upon arrival, but she had only managed to drag him a few feet. It would have to do. She hid in the kitchen and waited.

"Hey, Kev, Andrew and Dave are waiting in the car, where's the ba—"

There was a moment of silence then she heard Rob's heavy footsteps as he rushed across the living room. He had come alone then, which made her job slightly easier, but if things worked out well, it wouldn't be long before Andrew and Dave came looking for him.

"What the fuck?" came Rob's voice. "Oh shit, oh fuck, what did she do to you? Shit, shit!"

There was silence again then she heard his heavy breathing. "Sarah, what did you do? Are you here? Look, it's okay, I get it. He was a nasty fucker, he deserved what you did to him. Just come out and I swear I won't say or do anything. You can go. This has gone too far already. Just get outta here and run, I'll cover for you, say you'd already left when I came up."

Am I a Monster?

Funny how people tended to repeat the same as everyone else in times of trauma and stress. Try to lie or talk their way out of things. Rob almost sounded convincing. Both he and Kevin must think she was extremely stupid, naïve, or too far out of it to appreciate the ridiculous notion of their words. Later, if things worked as she hoped, Andrew would probably say exactly the same thing. Maybe even get down on his knees and beg for forgiveness, that he hadn't meant for things to go this far. Well, it was too late for that now because she sure as hell did intend on taking thing further than they could ever imagine.

She purposefully made a noise in the kitchen, scraping a chair to alert him. Either he would come barging in or creep in and try to surprise her. It didn't matter either way what he did. Despite her senses being pretty much destroyed in every way, she thought she could smell him as he approached, her back to him. Carrying body parts out to the middle of a field must have caused him to sweat more than usual.

"Sarah, I know you're in the kitchen. I just heard you. I hope you're not planning anything stupid. Kevin got what he deserved, I told you. I only did what I did because if not, well, you know what Andrew's like if he doesn't get his own way. I was gonna phone the police myself right after your father died. He didn't deserve that. So come on out and just get outta here."

He was standing right behind the closed door, no doubt debating whether to barge in or not. She jerked the chair again that was next to her. After a few seconds of silence, Rob must have lost his patience, because she heard the creaking of hinges as he opened the door. She took a deep breath, hurting her weakened lungs in the process.

"Sarah? You are in so much trouble you little bitch.

When Andrew sees what you've done, everything that happened to you before is nothing in comparison. I'm personally gonna cut your dirty little puss—"

A hand gripped her shoulder, ready to spin her around. But before that could happen, Sarah grabbed the boiling pot in front of her, turned and threw the contents over Rob. It might have been a second before he reacted until the pain hit him. Maybe he thought it was just water she'd thrown over him because in that brief instance a look of annoyance crossed his face. Then the boiling oil began to soak into his skin, bubbling away disintegrating the skin and boiling the flesh beneath.

He staggered back, hands and arms waving in the air as though in the throes of some religious fever. The oil melted away his eyelids, dripping onto his exposed eyeballs. His already greasy hair fell out in clumps. Blisters appeared like mushrooms all over his face, popping instantly and adding to the sticky, thick substance. Because he'd had his mouth open when she threw it, surely to continue spewing insults and threats, a large amount of oil had gone down his throat. She watched fascinated and in awe as Rob's tongue bubbled, reminding her of watching her father cook bacon on the grill, fat spitting everywhere. His tongue resembled that bacon. His lips melted, dangling in pieces from his face as though he'd bitten them off. Maybe he had because now he was screaming and howling, staggering backwards and crashing into the kitchen cupboards and walls.

Surely blind now, because his eyeballs were also melting and sliding down his cheeks, he spun around in circles, as his cheeks melted too leaving large gaps in his face. Eventually, he crumpled to the floor. Sarah stood over him, contemplating her options. If Andrew and Dave were waiting in the car, it wouldn't be long before

Am I a Monster?

one or both came looking for their friend. He wasn't quite dead yet either, more in shock, on the verge of being unconscious. She certainly didn't want him to live but the more she thought about, maybe this was more fitting. He would spend the rest of his life blind, disfigured and condemned to spend his sad existence in complete ostracism, shunned from the rest of the world. Someone—his parents maybe—might tell him the extent of his injuries and he might take it upon himself to commit suicide. If he had the courage, of course, which she doubted. And also, if he wasn't in prison once it was discovered his involvement in Sarah's kidnaping.

Yes, that was a much better punishment for him, but as an afterthought, she took out a knife from one of the drawers, cut away his jeans and castrated him too, popping his tiny little dick into his mouth as she had done to Kevin. If he didn't wish he was dead already, he would now.

Chapter 27

Ironically, Rob's semi-demise had very nearly been Sarah's too. After taking one last look at him as he fell into darkness—unconscious or dead, she didn't know—she slipped in the still-hot olive oil. She landed on her back, cracking the back of her head on the tiled floor and both elbows as she tried in vain to break her fall. But the adrenaline rush from attacking Rob had already worn off and she had been fragile again, not having the speed or strength to grab onto something.

After a few seconds of being dazed, a possible concussion, the pain in her elbows had woken her from her stupor. As she tried to sit up, her arms twisted unnaturally, and she was sure an agonising gnawing in her elbows meant she'd broken both arms. If she tried to move them just the slightest, she had to bite down on her tongue to stop herself from screaming out loud. But knowing she couldn't lay here all day or Dave or Andrew would find her, very tentatively, she moved one arm and checked. There was no jutting bone, no immediate discolouring of the skin or ominous lumps which suggested that perhaps she'd only chipped the bone or less. Still terribly painful but at least they weren't broken. Because if they had been soon it wouldn't be the only one. Andrew was going to be extremely pissed when he discovered Sarah had outwitted and beaten two of his friends.

Somehow, she managed to drag herself out of the kitchen without burning herself too much on the oil or slipping again and hobbled over to the window. When she looked out, she saw Dave getting out of a blue Escort and heading towards the building. It looked like it was

Am I a Monster?

Dave's turn next then.

She had mixed feelings about Dave. On the one hand, he was the only one of the four boys that seemed genuinely disgusted and perturbed by what they did to her. He'd raped her along with the others the first couple of days but there had been no particular joy it seemed on his behalf as he did it. It might have been because his girlfriend, Karen, had been present which in itself seemed weird, but perhaps Karen got off seeing her boyfriend with others. At the time it hadn't been something Sarah gave much thought to—she had more important things to worry about. He had been the one that frequented Andrew's flat the least too, and again, she had to assume it was because he already got his needs fulfilled elsewhere. The times when he was here, with or without Karen, he never participated in the fun and games unless obliged to do so, and was never the instigator, either.

It was later when Dave and Karen came to the flat to bring her the hamburger she had understood he was just frightened of Andrew like everyone else and was too scared to say or do anything to help. If he did, Andrew might take it out on Karen which apparently Andrew had after she gave her the tampon. So in that sense she could understand him. But on the other hand, Dave must be such a coward, such a pathetic individual he had stood back and done nothing even when Sarah had been forced to kill his girlfriend. Even helping to dismember then subsequently help dispose of the remains. If anything, if he truly loved Karen, he would have put his safety and even his own life at risk to prevent Karen from dying. But he hadn't. He could have ran straight from the flat to the police. Rob wasn't going to catch him and Kevin and Andrew had been too occupied with her and Karen. So this made him just as guilty when it came to Karen at least. He deserved the same execution as all the others.

She just had time to hide behind a door when Dave came in, grabbing a heavy glass ashtray as she did so. He never noticed her as he took in Kevin's mutilated body; instead, staring at it disbelievingly.

"Rob? Rob, you here? What the fuck happened? Did you do that to Kevin? And where's Sarah?"

He stepped further into the room and that was when Sarah used all her remaining strength to smash him over the back of the head with the ashtray. Her strength was fading already so all it did was cause him to stagger back, yelling in pain and clutch at his now bleeding head. She had been hoping it might knock him out so she could finish him off easier but it looked like it wasn't to be. She did have time to swing the ashtray at his face again though smashing his nose and breaking it instantly. That did the trick and he was soon semi-conscious on the floor. Her strength now almost gone completely, she slumped to the floor and grabbed a pair of scissors laying nearby. Within a few minutes, Dave was naked. Her idea had been to castrate him too, but then she noticed the vase with the roses in them that Karen had given him a few days earlier. Sarah had the perfect idea…

It was after she finished introducing the stem and burning with Dave's own cigarette lighter the tip of his penis that Andrew barged in, demanding to know why the hell they were taking so long.

Chapter 28

Sarah had just managed to pull herself to her feet when he walked in. They stood staring at each other for what seemed forever. Then Andrew glanced around the room at the carnage before him. When he looked back at Sarah, his face was twisted into a menacing sneer. His eyes looked like they were on fire. He was breathing so heavily he was foaming at the mouth, as though rabid. And Sarah guessed he probably was. His precious control and authority had been taken from him. And now, either one or both of them was going to die.

"Hi, Andrew, pleased to see me up and about at last? I've been doing the chores as you can see. Gathering up the trash. Took me quite a while but I think I did a good job. What do you think? Do I get another Big Mac as a treat?"

"How?" was all he seemed capable of saying.

"A combination of things, Andy. Can I call you Andy? You are my boyfriend, after all, right? It's amazing the amount of protein and calories a Big Mac has in it. That plus the sugar in the cola and the other stuff I found in your fridge. Plus, you forcing me to kill my own father, and then Karen…A pretty potent concoction. They all begged and cried like babies when I cut their dicks off, by the way. Rob is in the kitchen. I gave him a nice, hot shower. He needed it."

"But…but you should have been practically dead. Look at you, you look like a fucking emaciated zombie. There's no way you should have been able to overcome three men."

"The mind is a powerful tool, Andy. You of all people should know that. If there's a will, there's a way and all that."

"But…"

He looked in utter shock. His whole plan had gone to shit. He had to know now that he couldn't keep her alive here any longer. That she had somehow survived against the odds and he hadn't managed to break her completely. But as he looked around again and saw there were still black rubbish bags with other body parts still to remove, and now all those of his friends, he looked defeated. But Andrew was not the kind of kid to see things rationally. In his world, things ran smoothly and if they didn't he ensured they soon did again. Chaos was not an element to last very long.

Perhaps for that reason, he turned his attention back to Sarah. His hands curled into fists, the look of bewilderment and shock was replaced once again by rage.

"So you think it's over? You're just gonna walk out of here as if nothing happened? That I'm gonna let you go? Well, it's over for you, Sarah. You're gonna be joining your daddy out in Fritton Woods. I'll fucking cut you up myself, while you're still alive for what you did."

He charged her. Sarah was standing by the door to the spare bedroom where Dave lay sprawled. As he ran towards her, he pulled an arm back ready to punch her in the face, but just before he could launch it, Sarah ducked and stabbed him in the ribs with the scissors she had been holding behind her back. Andrew went flying to the floor, howling in pain. He tried to pull them out, but they were embedded pretty deeply and it was evidently too painful to do so. So she did it for him, retrieving them and then tried to sink the blades into his throat. But Andrew was too quick for her. He knocked her arm away causing her to drop the scissors.

Despite the blood that was soaking his shirt, he

Am I a Monster?

jumped up quicker than Sarah thought possible and kicked her between the legs. She grunted and doubled over, immense pain from an already severely injured area. The nail that had been used to pierce her vagina was displaced, almost torn from the delicate flesh. He made to kick her there again, hurling insults at her but she managed to turn over just in time. But it didn't make a lot of difference. His foot landed where the unhealed scars were on her back from the game of noughts and crosses they'd played there. Instantly, she felt the scars torn open and blood running down her back.

"Did you think you was gonna kill me too, Sarah? Gonna cut my balls off as well, after everything I did for you? Bitch!"

He brought his foot back to kick her again but with almost the last of her strength, she managed to grab the scissors and plunge them into the top of his Nike trainer. It amazed her where she was getting the strength from as she watched Andrew howl once more. She vowed that if she was getting out of this alive, she would sustain herself on Big Macs and Coke for the rest of her life. That plus the chocolate biscuits she'd found in the cupboard and the pie in the fridge before Kevin turned up.

Her groin was so sore and throbbing she could barely move her legs without a stab of agony shooting up her chest, but she somehow managed to grab onto the door handle and pull herself to her feet while Andrew hopped on one foot. When he bent down to pull the scissors out, Sarah hobbled off to the kitchen to look for another weapon. If anyone deserved castrating, it was Andrew.

"You fucking bitch! I'm gonna cut your fucking pussy out with these scissors, you slut!"

She was lightheaded, dizzy and on the verge of puking from the exertion but she made it to the kitchen and grabbed onto the sink before she collapsed. Andrew was coming after her already throwing insults and threats at her. She opened the top drawer beside the sink and pulled out the biggest knife she could find. Andrew burst into the kitchen holding the bloodied scissors in the air like a knife and headed straight for her. But he must have been so blind with rage, he never even noticed Rob's mutilated body on the floor and much less the slippery olive oil because just before he reached her, he skidded and fell down hard on his back, crashing onto the floor, his head landing on Rob's face, the scissors flying.

Sarah wasted no time. Careful not to slip herself, she hobbled over to Andrew who lay there stunned, and slammed the blade into his stomach as far in as it would go. Andrew winced and inhaled sharply. She pulled it out, ready to repeat the action when Andrew rolled off Rob's body and tried to stand up. But he was still unaware of the oil on the floor because his feet slipped out from under him again and this time he landed on his stomach, screaming as he did so.

He screamed again when he saw what was left of Rob's face, momentarily forgetting he'd been stabbed several times. He soon remembered though when Sarah, one hand gripping the kitchen surface so as not to slip and also because she couldn't squat anymore, leaned over and sank the blade straight into Andrew's mouth, as far in as it would go so it lodged at the back of his throat.

"Now that's what I call a deepthroat, Andy. Wouldn't you agree?" she said smiling and panting.

His eyes bulging, a grotesque choking, moaning sound coming from him, he tried to pull it out but as before the pain must have been too much for him. He looked up at her, pleading.

"You should have killed me before, Andy. You honestly thought you was going to keep me here forever,

Am I a Monster?

torturing and starving me, like I was your slave or something? You're sick. You probably know that as well. You probably convinced yourself you was doing the right thing. And all because I pushed you one night when you were being vulgar and drunk. Well, look what came of it. Funny how simple actions can lead to a greater good, isn't it?

"If it wasn't for you doing what you did, kidnapping me, then allowing me to live, you would probably have done it to someone else instead. Someone weaker than I am. So maybe after all you did, it's a blessing in disguise that some other poor unfortunate didn't have to go through all that.

"You see, Andy, you picked the wrong one. It's not the first time such a thing happened to me, so I was able to be strong, knowing you'd fuck up just like the last one did. And now you're going to pay for it."

Wincing, she struggled to squat beside him, feeling all the old scars open up again and wrenched the knife from his mouth.

"I was going to scoop your eyeballs first like I did to Rob, but I want you to watch. I've had to watch everything, Andy, and it wasn't a pretty sight. It's only fair wouldn't you agree."

He tried to say something but instead spluttered and spat out a spray of blood. There was plenty more pooling around him from the wounds to his mouth, ribs and foot. Sarah cut open his shirt then cut off the buttons of his jeans before pulling them down. He gripped her wrist but it was his turn to be the weakest now. His time of being in charge was over. She swiped it away like a pesky fly.

On his bare chest, she carved the word '*coward*', making sure the blade entered deep enough the scar would follow him to his grave. Then, she sat back and considered her options. Like Rob, she had to ask herself if dying was perhaps too good for him. Wouldn't suffering the rest of his pathetic life be a much more deserving punishment? He might like to think he was in control of everything but he would never find the courage to kill himself. It was beyond him. He was a coward as the carving on his chest said. Better to let him remember all the horrific things he had done forever, right? He wouldn't even go to the police and tell them what she did for fear of being implicated in the kidnapping and torture of Sarah. He'd remain here in this shitty little flat feeling pain and sorrow every single day, wishing he was dead but unable to fulfil his desires. Have to spend every single day in pain that not even the best painkillers could help with. Even when he slept he would be in pain.

Sarah left him there, knowing he was too weak to retaliate or escape and looked through the kitchen drawers and stopped when she pulled out the meat cleaver. Then she found a spray can of bug killer and took that along with a box of matches. But first she made herself a sandwich; she was learning that killing people was hard, tiring work. She returned to Andrew who had tried to pull himself up but failed dismally and eased herself to the floor again, eating her sandwich while watching him squirm.

"So, this is going to hurt okay, but don't worry, you'll live. I'll phone an ambulance myself after I've gone. Guess I should find some clothes first though, eh? Can I borrow yours? Thanks. You probably won't want to live after I finish but then, it's all about having control over one's life, isn't it? You taught me that one."

She finished her sandwich, wiped her decimated lips that she'd almost bitten off several times and held up the meat cleaver.

"Mmm, where to start?"

Am I a Monster?

It was easy really. She held the cleaver high and brought it down on his left wrist. After a little wiggling the blade came free and she did it again finally severing it. She repeated with the right. Then came the clever part.

"So we can't have you bleeding to death on us, can we? Of course not, Sarah. Good boy."

He was whimpering and squirming on the floor, tears running from his eyes, unable to speak. She figured he was in too much pain to do so. She took the can of bug killer, lit a match and when she pressed the trigger, she held the great flame to his bleeding wrists, soon cauterising them. The stench was intense, causing her to cough and gag herself. After just a few seconds of burning his wrists stopped bleeding.

"There, that's better. Now you won't be punching anyone ever again. Now for the next."

She repeated the same operation on both his ankles, cauterising them too.

"Now you can't kick anyone either, Andy. How do you feel? Hungry? Should I go grab us a Big Mac or something?"

His eyes flickered. It wouldn't be long before he passed out. His phone had rung several times and when she checked it, some guy's name she didn't recognise kept popping up. She went to the living room window and checked. The blue Escort had gone—she'd forgotten about that. Evidently, Andrew's friend had gotten tired of waiting. Another lucky break for her.

She returned to Andrew, lit the can again and gripped the tip of his penis. She held the flame against the tip and sealed the urethra by melting the flesh surrounding it. That brought a gargled scream from him as she had expected.

"And you won't be raping anyone ever again, either, Andy. One last thing and I'll get outta here."

She didn't want him entirely blind. She wanted him to appreciate things every day when he looked in his mirror so for the last time, held the flame to his left eyeball and melted it. Thick goo ran down his cheek as the eyeball popped. Sarah leaned over and kissed his other cheek.

"Time for me to go, Andrew. Thanks for everything. It's been a real eye-opener. Bye now."

She pulled herself to her feet and went to Andrew's bedroom where she found some suitable clothes then went to the bathroom to wash all the blood off her face. The first stop would be home, reuniting with her mother. That was going to be an emotional reunion if ever there was one. She wondered if her book deal was still on or had been cancelled. Not that it really mattered anymore. Sarah's dreams of living in a big mansion surrounded by kids and writing the next best-seller had vanquished along with everything else. She had new objectives now. Sarah took Andrew's mobile phone, spat in his face and left, closing the door gently behind her.

Am I a Monster?

Chapter 29

She didn't stop to speak to anyone on the way home, ignoring the comments and strange looks her way, some people making a wide berth or even crossing to the other side of the road. She knew she looked sick despite having washed her face, maybe a homeless girl, a drug addict. The burn marks from having a plastic bottle dripping onto her face were never going to go away and most of her hair was missing, just a few anarchic clumps here and there remaining. She staggered most of the way too, her broken feet never completely recovering. A few people stopped her to ask if she was okay, but she ignored those too, just wanting to get home as quick as possible. At the same time, something she thought she would never feel again yet had always taken for granted, and at the same time hated—the feel of the wind and drizzle on her face. As usual the sun was hiding but it didn't matter, it was enough to feel all the other elements on her skin. Things that everyone took for granted and never even noticed anymore she was seeing as though for the very first time and even though each step she took sent shockwaves up her body she still had a smile on her face.

And yet, she should have known these feelings because it wasn't the first time she had felt them. Once before, the exact same sensation of relief and an overwhelming joy at being alive again had coursed through her veins. Unfortunately, the gods had deemed it necessary she suffer through it all once more.

Sarah arrived home and almost ran into the door. Because it wouldn't open when she tried the handle. She rang the bell several times, then peered through the living room window and saw nothing. She then realised to her shock and horror that she was now the only person who knew where her father was. They were probably still out looking for him, same as they had with her. Her mother would be in utter shock, having lost first her daughter, then her husband. She was probably not even here, guaranteed to be at Sarah's aunt or someplace. Sarah's initial idea had been to say nothing about her ordeal, saying she didn't know where she had been kept, but how could she not reveal what happened to her own father?

This was something she was going to have to think about long and hard because no matter what ordeal she had been through, if the police found the boys' bodies, there was a good chance self-defence might not be enough to save her from prison. And that was not going to happen. Her first thought upon escaping had been screaming for help. Slumping to the ground and waiting for someone to call the police and an ambulance, but another thought had occurred to her. What if she was arrested for murdering the boys? Could she really claim self-defence? Considering what she had done to them, she wasn't so sure. The defence barrister would say they had suffered terribly, that there had been no need to put them through that regardless of the fact they had done similar things to her. He might suggest she was a monster, that she needed to be locked up in Northgate forever. And the thought made her wonder; *am I a monster*? Were her actions justified? Was '*an eye for an eye*' legitimate in this case?

Still stunned about her father, she remembered there was a spare key under the mat by the door, found it and let herself in. It also occurred to her that both hers and her father's disappearance had been nationwide news, yet on the way home no one it seemed had recognised

Am I a Monster?

her. She must look worse than she thought. The fact she'd lost more than double her body weight obviously helped. And in a way, she was glad she hadn't been stopped.

As expected, when she entered the house was silent. Dust gathered on the staircase which meant no one had been home for a while. She thought of using her spare mobile phone to try and contact her mother, desperate to give her both good and bad news, then she thought of Shelly who had told her all that time ago that Andrew seemed a nice kid. What had she thought when Sarah disappeared? No doubt she, like everyone else, assumed Sarah was dead. She wanted to phone all her friends, relatives and loved ones, but first she needed to rest a little. A hot bath to gently wipe the blood off. A hospital visit would be in order too. A long stay there for sure. The crude piercings done to her breasts and vagina still caused terrible throbbing, aching pains in her body. Not to mention the probable internal damage. It was highly unlikely but she could be pregnant too. But for now, if only for ten minutes, she just wanted to be alone with her thoughts, consider what she was going to tell the police.

Several ideas ran through her mind. Make something to eat; something strong like a vodka and coke for her nerves; a bar of chocolate or surely there had to be some of her favourite biscuits laying about somewhere. She could happily eat a whole packet right now. Anything just to feel a semblance of normality again. But instead, she decided on a hot bath before phoning the police and ambulance. Shed a few tears for her father and mother too.

A few minutes later she eased herself into the water, that simultaneously stung the multiple scars on her body yet refreshed her at the same time. As predicted, while she lay back and closed her eyes the memories of everything that had happened to her, being forced to kill her own father, came flooding back and she wept. She would give anything to bring her father back, give her own life if that was what it took. After everything he and his family had been through, it wasn't fair he should die like this. Because it wasn't the first time he had rescued her from a similar predicament.

Six years ago, her father had rescued her from a fellow detective's basement after she was kidnapped. The man, Clive Watson, had sliced several lengths of flesh from her arm then cooked and ate them. He did the same to several other kids too until Sarah's dad finally found her in a hidden part of the basement. Clive was now in Northgate Hospital for the Criminally Insane, never to be released again. Her father, Jeff, had stepped down from being a detective to just being a regular officer, then decided they should all assume pseudonyms and move to another village to avoid the onslaught of journalists and morbid sightseers. Every day there was a knock on the door from people wanting to interview her and her parents. True-crime fanatics wanting to hear every single detail about her suffering. Vast sums of money offered to record a documentary or have her story told in a book. It had gone on for weeks afterwards, Sarah hiding in her room, too scared to venture outside unless she was being whisked to hospital for more skin transplants in total secrecy. Eventually her parents had cracked under the strain and Jeff had come up with a plan. Sarah had died at the hospital from her injuries and the immense shock to her system and it had worked, the calls stopped coming. She had been Sophie back then, an innocent ten-year-old, the whole world before her, and it had been cruelly stolen from her. And now it had just happened all over again.

But this time, she wasn't going to just sit back and let

Am I a Monster?

it overwhelm her. This time, unlike the countless hours of therapy and skin transplants to hide the burns she had required when all she had wanted to do was curl up and die, this would make her stronger. If what didn't kill you made you stronger was a popular saying, this time she was going to take it to a more literal level. The likes of Andrew Foreman and his cronies weren't going to get away with this anymore. And she wasn't going to let the police intervene either. The force had already lost one good man; they weren't going to lose another. This time, she would take matters into her own hands. She thought she had a lot of practice at it by now. *Maybe I am a monster*, she wondered. *But if so, so are they all.*

When at home, Andrew liked to watch the news, keep updated on the search for Sarah. She had barely been conscious enough to be aware of what was happening in the world but one thing she did remember now was that a series of brutal murders had taken place on nearby Green Lake. Men viciously tortured for prolonged spells, then mutilated and dismembered, their remains in many cases thrown into the lake and pecked at by the many fish there. It had been a woman that did it, Claire Peterson, confessing to all the crimes in revenge, she said, for all the humiliation she had been put through her entire life. Sarah could empathise with her. To Sarah, this sounded like a plan. A very good one. To the point she thought about going to visit her later in nearby Northgate Hospital for the Criminally Insane. For research, of course.

Wiping the tears from her face, Sarah climbed out of the bathtub, wrapped herself in a thick, soft towel and headed downstairs to phone for the police and an ambulance.

<u>The End</u>

Author's Notes

Well, you made it. Happy? Everything you hoped for and more? I was halfway through writing this when I had a sudden idea; what if Sarah is really Sophie from, They Are All Monsters? Kinda like a follow-up story. Sounded fun. Did you guess it was her? I hope you enjoyed it because that means all the hard work paid off. Not to mention the hours and hours of YouTube documentaries I watched over the last few months to try and understand why some of the most evil, vile people on the planet did such things in real life. It wasn't pleasant. Some of the things I watched were so terrible, if it came from a fictional novel, people wouldn't believe it, much less the victim surviving as is the case with Sarah here. Well, let me tell you right now, they're wrong. The will to survive is an amazing thing.

I had a discussion with a friend regarding this book during its early stages saying it seemed highly unlikely Sarah could possibly survive such abuse. The answer I gave her is a shorter version of the one I'm now going to give you just as I did with the previous book, They Are All Monsters.

Suzanne Caper was a 17-year-old English girl. She had a tough upbringing. Her dad left when she was young and her mother remarried soon afterwards, but the relationship between her mother and stepfather was toxic to say the least. It meant there was always fighting going on in the household and neither had any time for her, to the point the mother just walked out one day leaving Suzanne with her sister and stepfather. So, as she grew up she was an extremely lonely girl, the only thing she

Am I a Monster?

ever wanted in life was to be loved. She thought she found it in neighbour, Jean Powell, who lived with five others that would come and go.

They soon took advantage of Suzanne's vulnerable character and desire to do anything she could to appease and be loved when she moved in with them. Over the course of the next 6 weeks or so, they raped and beat her daily, using all manner of objects including ornaments and decorative 3ft long wooden spoons. They beat her so badly her left arm was rendered useless. She was starved, often going days without food and water. She was tied spreadeagled to an old bed, missing the mattress, so for five days she had the wooden boards and the springs digging into her back, no use of a toilet so she lay in her own urine and faeces.

Headphones were put over her ears and techno music played on repeat at full volume all night. She was injected with amphetamine to avoid her losing consciousness and making sure she was awake all night with that music blaring in her ears over and over. She was made to eat her own faeces. Her teeth were pulled out with pliers. There came a point there was not a single area on her body free from scars and bruises. Cigarettes were stubbed out on her eyeballs.

All this went on daily from all five people for about 6 weeks until they decided they should kill her for fear of being caught. They took a barely alive Suzanne to a field, doused her in lighter fluid, set her on fire and laughed as they walked away leaving her to burn to death.

But…

Somehow, Suzanne managed to put out the flames, crawl up an embankment and flag down a passing car. In hospital, she was able to describe what they did to her and give their names. She died a week later.

You can find this case easily enough on YouTube, but

for me the most tragic of all this is that she managed to survive long enough to get help. She almost made it. Why did they do this to her? They never said. It seemed they did so because they were bored and it was fun.

So yes, that was tough to watch. Why do it then, you ask. Because I want(ed)to know the reasons why if I was going to write about this stuff. What could lead a seemingly normal person to cause such atrocities on another human being? After watching probably 30 or 40 cases of torture to other humans, I'm still left with the question. Having control over others seems to be the most common excuse, as is the case with Andrew in this book. They are able to justify what they do because they had a shitty upbringing and it's all the world's fault, not theirs. Payback, in other words.

Sarah asks herself if what she did was justified. Is she a monster just like they were? Personally, I think she was more than justified. Unfortunately, the criminal system often thinks otherwise, but, of course, those wonderful folks have never been through the kinds of things Sarah did, not to mention the suffering from her parents.

I hope you enjoyed reading this book. In places I didn't enjoy writing it and there are scenes I was going to add but refrained from doing so. Sarah suffered enough, right? So yes, these things do happen and worse. There could be (and probably is) someone right now, tied to a bed, being raped and beaten and tortured senseless as you read this, wishing they were dead, praying to be found.

If you did or didn't enjoy it, please leave a review on Amazon. It's gold for us indie authors and means so much. A simple sentence is enough; on Amazon it's a numbers game.

As always, I would like to thank a number of people who read this book, either during its early days, or as

Am I a Monster?

ARC readers. In no particular order: Shannon Zablocki, Emily Lasater, Tracey Nudd, Leah Dawn Cole, Shannon Etarra, Stefanie Duncan, Melissa Trevino, Kay Victoria, Danielle Yeager, Donna VC, Nicole Burns, Jennifer Horgan, Nancy Sienna Sundquist, Corrina Morse, Carol Howley, Chandra Marie, Tasha Schiedel, Steph Kneeland, Katrina Peirson, Josette Thomas, Monica Granado, Heidi Daniels, David John, Michael Livingstone, Stephanie Evans, Marie-France Brunet, Emily Haynes, Amanda Frost, Wendy Latham, Margaret Hamnett, Tanya Mari, Derek Thomas. Thank you all so much for helping out!

J. Boote

ALSO BY J. BOOTE

Man's Best Friend
Love You To Bits
Buried
They are all Monsters

ALSO BY JUSTIN BOOTE

Short Story Collections:

Love Wanes, Fear is Forever
Love Wanes, Fear is Forever: Volume 2
Love Wanes, Fear is Forever: Volume 3

Novels:

Serial
Combustion
Chasing Ghosts
Carnivore: Book 1 of The Ghosts of Northgate trilogy
The Ghosts of Northgate: Book 2 of The Ghosts of Northgate trilogy
A Mad World: Book 3 of The Ghosts of Northgate trilogy
The Undead Possession Series –
Book 1: Infestation
Book 2: Resurrection
Book 3: Corruption
Book 4: Legion
Book 5: Resurgence

From Wicked House Publishers:

Am I a Monster?
    In Grandma's Room (a YA horror novel)

Short stories available on Godless

Badass
Grandmother Drinks Blood
If Flies Could Fart
A Question of Possession

Printed in Great Britain
by Amazon